Western
Havill β

FEB 4   1986

Timber Blood.

TIMBER BLOOD

By the Same Author

The Killer
The Worst Enemy
Leadfire

TIMBER BLOOD

Steven Havill

Walker and Company
New York

First published in the United States of America
in 1985 by the Walker Publishing Company, Inc.

Published simultaneously in Canada by John Wiley & Sons
Canada, Limited, Rexdale, Ontario.

Library of Congress Cataloging-in-Publication Data

Havill, Steven.
  Timber blood.

    I. Title.
PS3558.A785T5 1985   813'.54   85-15525
ISBN 0-8027-4052-9

Printed in the United States of America

10 9 8 7 6 5 4 3 2 1

14.95

For Eric and Mark, and for Kathleen

TIMBER BLOOD

I

WITHOUT a cloud of moisture in sight, Bert Schmidt should have been able to look down from the crown of Williams Peak and eyeball more than ten thousand square miles of territory. But on that early November day in 1886, the clouds spread over the country in long, gray-blue wisps that hugged the ground and crept up the narrow valleys. Further distant, where the green-blanketed hills gave way to the open prairie, haze blended land with sky, smudging the colors of both to an even dullness. Prairie fires had swept across the drought-stricken ranges, gobbling up precious forage. The acrid smoke from the fires hung heavy in the air. It choked the cowpunchers who fought first one blaze and then another. It stung their eyes and clung to their clothes. For three months, the smoke had been a part of their everyday lives.

Schmidt's money didn't lie with the lowlands, or with the cattle, but the range fires concerned him nonetheless. His horse stamped a foot and the duff under the animal's hoof fairly crackled. Not just the prairies were tinder. Williams Peak, touching ten thousand feet where Schmidt then rested, and all of its brethren both greater and lesser, were towering reservoirs of fuel, waiting for a spark. And, Schmidt reflected ruefully, the drought had lasted since June.

Before that, during the winter months of '85 and '86, heavy snows had crushed the pine and fir boughs with such force that each tree looked like a tall icicle, arrow slender. The loggers struggled and cursed the sleds, cursed the big horses who blew out clouds of steamy breath as they strug-

1

gled against the snow, cursed the logs that snowballed as they rolled and became impossible to handle.

That spring the run-off from the winter storms turned Schmidt's logging roads into knee-deep quagmires where chains snapped with ease and horses went down with shrill whinnies of fright and pain. The logs reached Schmidt's mill coated with heavy mud that dried to the consistency of concrete. He had set four men to chipping the logs almost clean but still the big teeth of the steam-powered saw howled and spat clay shrapnel as the logs were forced up the saw carriage.

Bert Schmidt could live with all that. From time to time, his broad, strong face went grim with the headache of it all, but he still made his fortune. What he feared most was what he was watching that late afternoon in November. If the trees were standing, he could harvest them, come snow, mud, bitter cold, or loggers who left the mountain seeking some easier way to earn thirty dollars a month. But Schmidt could not harvest blackened stumps. That summer alone, fire had denied Schmidt more than ten thousand acres.

He sat quietly on his horse and looked down at the smoke. There was a blaze over by Sutton Creek, twenty miles south and west. The smoke hugged the creek and stretched down the broad valley to the south. Ten miles further west, another curtain hung over the prairie where most of the Triple S cattle herded. To the east, partially obscured by the broad, flat back of Mount Bailey, a gray-blue tower hung in the air. Schmidt touched the reins and his horse obediently turned a small circle. There were fires to the north too, where one great cloud of smoke spread into an anvil that darkened fifty miles of prairie.

Even though Schmidt's men had fought perhaps fifty hot spots that summer and early fall, and desperately fought the mammoth blaze on Mount Bailey's flank, they had been lucky. To be harvesting so late in the season without snow, to be entering the eventual chill of this November without a trace of white was a near miracle. Schmidt's foremen had pushed the crews hard, hoping to build up a stockpile of saw logs that would hold over the winter. The days were hot. The temperature still reached the eighties when the sun was high. At night, the air chilled to nearly freezing, but the ground stayed dry.

Let the others talk of how early the geese had been seen veeing their way south two months before, Schmidt thought. Let them talk of a hard winter coming. The saw logs were piling up, stacked twenty feet high and more, awaiting the saws. When the timbers were cut—clean and white and fragrant—they would be stacked high again, this time on flatcars that waited behind Schmidt's locomotive. The narrow-gauge track wound down from his mill above the village of Williams and then shot south to the main line that ran across the young state from east to west. The locomotive, with black boiler, silver shafts, and gold filigree, would sit by the mill until there was a break in the dryness. With the stack belching black smoke and fountains of sparks, the engineer might have been able to draw one load of lumber down the mountain before the engine turned the trees along the way into flame.

"Son of a bitchin' weather," Schmidt mumbled. He urged his horse into a lazy walk that took them through the tall timber, down the hill trail and into Williams. By the time he tied his horse in front of Mike Buchanan's emporium, his shirt clung wetly to his broad back and chafed under his arms. A sawyer beetle had clung to his collar, Schmidt flicked it off into the dust, slapping his trousers with his narrow-brimmed hat as he went inside.

Big Mike Buchanan—all mouth, Schmidt thought, noticing that Buchanan was holding court at the bar. When Schmidt entered, the barman was standing with his ham-like hands spread a yard apart on the polished, thick pine slab that ran sixteen feet down one side of the room. Although Buchanan's emporium sold everything from rifles to knitting needles, it was the liquor that made Buchanan wealthy—this and a keen mind that saw profit in anything, if sold at the right time for the right price to the right person. The saloon was separated from the rest of the emporium by a stout wall that confined the noise and occasional roughhousing. Buchanan was shrewd enough to know that the ladies, sorting through the latest fabrics next door, wouldn't like to hear about it, or smell it.

"Lemme put it this way," Buchanan was saying as Schmidt came in. He looked over and saw the lumberman and, without stopping his chatter, reached for another glass and slid it down the bar where it stopped, as if trained, directly in front of Schmidt. Buchanan picked up a bottle but continued talking to the three men who stood at his bar. "What would you do if someone snuck up and swiped some . . . some . . ." he searched for the right example. "Some squash." He stood up straight, nearly six feet three, barrel-chested and heavy-maned with curly black hair. He spread his arms wide, the bottle of whiskey in one hand. "Huh? Some damn' squash. Say a good armful." The man to whom he was speaking looked skeptical. Buchanan's arms were full of the imaginary squash, and he patiently held them while he waited for an answer. "Huh? What wouldja do?"

"That ain't hardly the same thing," the man said. He looked over at his partners, then down the bar at Schmidt. "Howdy, Bert." Schmidt nodded and waited quietly.

"Is too."

"I don't see how it can be. Squash don't equal beef."

Buchanan leaned on the bar once more and his voice sank into deep tones of conciliation. "But don't you see, Ike, they do." Schmidt wondered where the conversation had started. "Them squash are part of your livelihood, aren't they? Man steals your squash, don't he steal your livelihood? Steal enough of 'em, along with maybe some corn and spuds and such, and ain't he starvin' you to death?"

"Well, I suppose so."

Buchanan sensed victory of sorts and grinned. "There now. All I'm saying is that in some ways, they're equals. Would you hang a man who up and filched an armload of your squash? Course you wouldn't," he said, stepping all over the other man's attempts at interruption. "So, it ain't fair that a man be hung for taking a mangy cow or two, from a herd that numbers maybe twenty thousand. Hell, that'd be like you hanging a man for takin' one kernel of corn from a whole row. That make sense to you?" He started to sidle toward Schmidt and the empty glass, but he still waited for an answer from his opponent.

The man shrugged. Buchanan turned to Schmidt and uncorked the bottle with one deft twist of his hand. He held the cork between his fingers like a stubby cigar.

"Warm out, ain't it?" he asked Schmidt. Before he could pour, Schmidt put his hand over the small glass. "Thought you said you wanted a drink?"

"Haven't said a thing," Schmidt said with an easy smile. "You're the one doing all the jawing." He took his hat off and laid it on the bar. Buchanan looked at it distastefully. "You got any ice left?" Schmidt asked. He took out a sodden bandana and mopped his dirty face with it, then stuffed it back in his pocket.

Buchanan's shaggy eyebrows shot up. "Course I got ice." Behind his emporium and stables, Buchanan had paid a half dozen luckless prospectors and out-of-work loggers to excavate the rocky hillside. The fortress that had been built in that hole held his real treasures—great chunks of ice sawed out of Tulley Lake when it froze all but solid during the deep winter months. Buchanan packed twenty or thirty tons of the crystal gold into his icehouse each year, burying it under mounds of sawdust. The logs that formed the walls had been purchased from Schmidt, and teams of oxen had hauled the logs down to the village. First logs, then dirt, until Buchanan's ice house sported walls nine feet thick and a roof covered with sod to a depth of five feet. He built great, castle doors wide enough to back a wagon through.

"Then I want some of that ice," Schmidt said. "I want me a glass of iced tea."

"Iced tea?"

"You bet," Schmidt said. He folded his hands like a man praying.

"Well, then," Buchanan said, "I ain't got no ice right here. I usually don't bring none in until after dinner, cause it melts." He hesitated as if that astounding scientific information would make a difference.

"Mike, you hoard ice like most men hoard gold. I know it isn't the dinner hour, or the weekend, or some special occasion, but I want some iced tea. And I'll pay."

Buchanan nodded and wiped his hands on a bar cloth. "It'll take a minute," he said. "Any of you fellas want some iced tea?"

The three shook their heads. One of them said, "Whiskey's cheaper," because he knew Mike Buchanan didn't give his ice away, even with winter just around the corner. The way the weather was, ice brought a premium. Buchanan bent down and lifted a shallow metal pan out from behind the bar. Inside it, an ice pick rattled.

"Be back directly," he said.

While he was gone, Schmidt began the ritual of packing his pipe. One of the men asked, "How's things on the mountain?"

"Dry and hot, like everywhere else. Got thunderheads brewing to the northwest, though. Maybe it'll rain this time."

The man scoffed. "It ain't ever gonna rain again in these parts, I don't think."

"You hear about the lynching?" a second man asked. He leaned forward to look at Schmidt.

"No."

"Well, there was one. They hung Luke Everett."

"Who the hell is Luke Everett?"

"Drifter . . . I heard he worked for you one season."

"Couldn't prove it by me. Don't remember the name. Whose beef he rustle?"

"Sam Averill's. They say one of the range detectives caught him red-handed. They say he fetched up hangin' from one of them cottonwoods down by Sutton Creek." The man took a sip of his whiskey. "Makes the fourth one this year I heard about. Not all around here, 'course."

Schmidt nodded noncommittally. "That what Mike was goin' on about when I came in?"

"Yep," replied the first man. "He don't think it's right, hanging a man for rustling."

"Nobody forces a man to rustle," Schmidt said.

"That's what I was tryin' to tell him. Cattle's the life blood of this country." The man grinned and leaned forward to look at Schmidt again. "That and saw logs, eh?"

Mike Buchanan came back inside. A handful of ice lay in the pan. He slid the pan nonchalantly onto the bar. "There we are," he announced. He selected a large glass from the shelf and clanked three angular chunks into it. "The tea," he said. Schmidt nodded and watched the ice as it began to melt against the side of the glass. Buchanan hefted a brown crock and poured the dark liquid into the glass. The ice cracked and popped.

"That tea left over from last spring?" Schmidt asked.

"Hell, I made it yesterday." He was lying through his teeth, and both of them knew it, but it made no difference. He watched the tea come up to the lip of the glass, and then Buchanan put the jug down on the shelf behind him. Schmidt reached for the glass, which was already cold to the touch. He took a long, deep drink and sighed. It was bitter and much too strong, but it was cold, and Schmidt grinned. "Just right."

"That'll be a dollar," Buchanan said as Schmidt drained the glass. Sediment coated the ice in the bottom.

"Now I'll have a beer," Schmidt said. "Right on top of that ice."

In between drinks, Schmidt slapped money on the bar without giving Buchanan the pleasure of hearing a complaint about the stiff price. When the last of the beer was gone, the lumberman sucked on the ice.

"When you going to be able to bring in my coal?" Buchanan asked.

"When I can run my engine without setting the mountain on fire," Schmidt replied. "You may have to wait for the first snow."

"Well, the yard's ready."

"I see it is. You built yourself another fortress."

"Anything for a buck," one of the others said.

"You wait," Buchanan said. "Come winter—specially if we have one like last year—folks are going to be cryin' for that coal."

"With all the firewood around?"

"Nothin' burns like coal," Buchanan said sagely. "There ain't no firewood made that'll burn the whole night long, like coal does. No sir. That's what folks'll pay for—not havin' to get up to stoke the pot. Isn't that right, Bert?"

"You're the expert," Schmidt replied.

"Besides, this is going to be one hell of a winter. I can feel it in my bones,"

"In your purse, you mean," Schmidt grinned.

Buchanan was about to protest with the doors swung open and a short, nondescript man entered, mopping his face. He was starting to go bald on top, and combed his long hair over the spot. He settled next to Schmidt and slapped the logger lightly on the shoulder. Of the six men then in the saloon, he was the only one wearing a gun. Pinned to the left breast of his sweaty shirt was a metal badge. It was well worn, but the lettering was deeply cut—"Tulley" across the top and arcing underneath, "Marshal."

"Here it is the fifth of November," he said, "and so hot a

man can't hardly breath. That and the damned smoke. Got fires all over hell. Gimme a beer, Mike."

Schmidt was mildly surprised to see the Tulley village marshall fifteen miles from home on such a hot day, and so late in the afternoon to boot. Tulley had grown enough for Jim Markham to carry a badge. Whether the former miner was an effective lawman was undecided. Schmidt knew it was only a matter of time before Williams would also hire a marshall. Schmidt didn't object to that, as long as the money to pay the officer didn't come out of Schmidt's own pocket. He had yet to see the quarrel, argument, or outright brawl that he or his foreman couldn't settle.

"What's this about Luke Everett, Jim?" Buchanan asked. "Is it true he got himself hung?"

"It's true," Markham said expressionlessly. "Mike, why'n hell don't you keep this beer of yours in that ice house, so's it stays cold? Christ, this is warm as piss."

"If he did that, nobody'd buy his ice," one of the others said.

"No, but he could charge more for the beer, and it'd be worth drinkin'," Markham observed.

"Everett working alone?" Buchanan asked, ignoring the barbs.

"Far as I know."

"That range dick catch him, like we heard?"

"Cyrus Taber? Yup, that's the way the story goes. No real proof, of course."

"You wasn't out there, too?"

Markham shook his head and took another swig of the tepid beer. "Nah. That ain't my stampin' ground. Taber caught Everett on Triple S land, I hear. Even had one of the Triple S foremen with him."

"How many'd he have?" Buchanan asked.

"How many'd who have?"

"Everett. How many beef?"

"I hear he had three, but you know the talk. They say he

was butcherin' one when they rode up on his campfire. Stupid fool was tryin' to work at night. Never saw them comin'. Tried to make a fight of it. Got himself hung right away. That's what I hear." He grinned and showed bad teeth. " 'Course, no one saw for sure who nabbed him. Talk has it that it was Taber and the foreman, Burke. No one has any way to prove it. How's things on the mountain, Schmidt?" Markham then asked.

"Hot, dry." Schmidt repeated the expected. He sighed and pulled out his pocket watch. The afternoon was about shot. "First time I can remember we had horses go down from the heat this time of year. Think it will ever break?"

"Who the hell knows," Markham said. "This heat keeps up, old Mike here ain't going to have much ice next year."

"Hey, you know what I hear?" Buchanan said, excitement quickening his words. "I heard by way of one of them newspapers I get that they've been shippin' ice all the way around the Horn, then freightin' it inland from Frisco. They say they cut it out of the Kennebec country in Maine. Ain't that something?"

"Lot of money in that," Markham observed.

Buchanan's chest swelled with pride. "My way's cheaper, by a sight."

"Unless Tulley Lake don't freeze," Schmidt said with a smile. "Then you're going to have to do the same thing."

"Ain't no chance of Tulley Lake not freezin'. Not this year. Not any year."

"I guess not," Schmidt agreed. "Winter'll come soon enough." He stood up to leave. "Winters and beef rustlers . . . this country will never be rid of 'em."

"We'll work at the one," Markham said quietly.

Schmidt chuckled. "Just don't hang 'em in my trees, Jim. Spooks the horses, makes 'em edgy. Keep your lynchings down on the flat, where they belong."

Bert Schmidt left the saloon and left the other men to their talk. As he rode slowly up the steep slope that was the main wagon rut of Williams, he didn't give more than a minute's thought to the talk about rustlers. From the front porch of his neat and compact cabin that perched a hundred yards north of the looming shadow of the sawmill, he could look over Williams and the prairies beyond. And when he did that, and heard the scream of the steam-driven saw that made the mill seem like a living thing, and when he smelled the fragrance of the freshly-cut lumber that was piled higher than his cabin, he felt like he owned the world.

II

CYRUS Taber had said more than once that he could smell rustlers at work. The morning of November 15 dawned cold and dreary. A wind from the northwest stirred through the dry pine boughs, the cold seeping into Taber's skin, starting down at his feet and working up. He took one hand off the saddlehorn to draw his sheepskin greatcoat tighter, then ducked his chin in an effort to stop the breeze from chilling his throat. He had read somewhere that the grippe started there and he was in no mood to be sick. He was hunting. And even though he couldn't smell the rustler, he could see him.

Taber's horse stood stock still, her breath issuing from wide nostrils in gentle curls. During her five years, she had been trained to do two things superbly—stand so still she seemed petrified, and flash into a full gallop on cue. So thorough and unrelenting had been her training that as she stood there, in the cover of the trees above the prairie north of Sutton Creek, her haunch muscles were bunched with expectation, like a jackrabbit tensed for flight.

The man on her back, Cyrus Taber, thirty-six years old and lean, waited almost as patiently and quietly. His fur cap was pulled down low and touched the tips of his small ears and the tops of his eyebrows. He surveyed the prairie from blue eyes that one man once had said reminded him of north country ice. Wisps of thin, blond hair touched the collar of his sheepskin. His spade-shaped beard was neatly trimmed. He had a sparse moustache whose ends were lost in the beard.

Taber was uncomfortable, but that was what he was paid for. This time, it was Sam Averill, owner of the Triple S

13

ranch to the south, who had pledged two hundred dollars for each rustler Taber caught. No questions were asked about how the catching was done, and Taber had a reputation for catching rustlers in the act: When he brought in a man, that man was guilty, and Taber was paid. Most of the two hundred that had been Luke Everett's life still rested in Taber's pocket, in a small deerskin purse. Taber took no joy in the killing. Rather, it was the waiting and then the chase that made his blood flow. In the past, he had worked the big, open ranges west and north where the herds moved in great, black masses that defied counting. Those massive herds attracted thieves and the hunting had been good. With winter coming, Taber was working south toward the major railheads where hot meals, hot baths, and soft beds could be found. He had been mildly surprised at Sam Averill's insistence when he first met him. But then, Taber had mused, one mangy steer seemed like the entire herd to a rancher. When one was taken, blood ran high.

Frequently, the ranchers never knew their beef was missing. Head tallies were seldom so accurate that five, ten, or even fifty steers taken from a herd of 5,000 would be missed. Taber knew that, as did all the ranchers. If rustlers weren't caught in the act, the simple truth was that they wouldn't be caught at all. What rubbed salt into the ranchers' wounds were the occasional carcasses left behind, evidence that the rustlers had enjoyed beef over their campfires.

That morning, the man who Cyrus Taber watched so patiently was a rank amateur. The range detective felt faintly sorry for him, although pity was not an emotion Taber allowed himself in excess. The rustler's luck had started bad and would stay that way. Taber was lucky to have been walking his horse through the timber nearby when the single rifle shot echoed across the prairie. It might have come from an elk hunter, a deer hunter, or even a murderer. For any of those, Cyrus Taber wouldn't have turned a hair. But from nearly five hundred yards away, he had seen the steer stumble sideways, take three or four staggering steps, then slide to its knees. The other cattle milled stupidly, and several trotted away. The thunder of the single shot died away, and Taber's pulse quickened. He pulled his palomino mare to an immediate halt. Nerves and muscles tense, they waited.

As Taber watched, the wounded steer kicked to its feet. It lurched a few steps, then thudded heavily onto its side, its legs working like those of a crushed insect. After a time, the steer lay quiet. From the shadows of the trees further down the gentle slope, a man appeared leading a horse.

"Ah," Taber breathed, watching intently. The man approached the steer, then stopped. He stood off a few yards. Taber could see the man's head turning. He was looking out across the vast prairie. There was nothing but cattle and emptiness. Taber's beard twitched as a thin smile curled his lips. Finally, moving quickly, the man tied a lariat to the hind legs of the dead animal and remounted his horse. The steer wasn't large, but even so, the horse missed its footing as the weight of the steer twanged the rope. Taber watched as the man urged his horse toward the protection of the trees.

"A sod buster," Taber muttered. "Meat for the table." The man halted his horse at the edge of the timber. Although a fair distance separated Taber from the rustler, and Taber had to peer around several trees, still he could see clearly. The man began working on a hindquarter.

Taber touched the palomino's sides ever so gently with his spurs and the horse's ears rotated. The range detective made a faint squeaking noise with his lips and the palomino stepped forward. He kept the animal in the trees, guiding her carefully around deadfalls and low-hanging limbs. Even though they moved slowly, the horse seemed able to sense Taber's excitement, for she chose her steps carefully. They meandered thus until only a hundred yards separated them from the rustler, still intent on his work. Taber checked the reins and the palomino stopped instantly, nostrils flaring. He stroked her neck, mumbling sweet nothings in her erect ears, and then he slid the carbine from the saddle boot. The gun was loaded and ready. He merely had to thumb the small spur hammer back. Had the rustler looked up then, had he looked toward the trees above him, he would have seen horse and rider poised. He did not look up until he heard the heavy pounding of hooves, and by then it was too late.

The palomino mare covered the hundred yards in seconds, and in one sense, the rustler was lucky. He had time only to stand and stare stupidly, rooted in place as the bearded rider swept down on him. He had no time to race to his own horse and grab his rifle. That saved his life.

Taber pulled the palomino up sharply. Her hooves scattered dirt and gravel against the hide of the dead steer.

"Morning," Taber said casually, as if his sudden appearance was nothing extraordinary. His face was as devoid of expression as the other man's was filled with apprehension. Taber sat his horse, silently regarding the man. The range detective's shrewd mind had already categorized the rustler as an amateur. He was dressed in cheap, flannel clothing, much worn. His ragged coat was buttoned tightly against the weather. The man wore no gun that Taber could see, but then, few did. A handgun cost a month's pay and was a luxury for most, worthless for anything but shooting your bolting horse to keep it out of a stampede, or for shooting men at very close range. This man didn't look the part of either a cowhand or a gunman. He looked like what he was, Taber thought—a weary, hungry, scared farmer. The man had good reason to be frightened, the detective thought grimly. He hadn't even worked up enough gumption to reply to Taber's greeting.

"You must work for Mister Averill?" Taber asked pleasantly. The muzzle of the rifle didn't waver an inch from the man's belly. A flicker of something akin to hope passed swiftly across the man's face, then vanished.

"No, I . . . I, ah . . ."

"That would be one of Mister Averill's stock, don't you think?" The brand of the Triple S was an obvious triple gash on the flank of the dead steer.

"You're . . ."

Taber waited a moment for the man to finish his sentence, and when the words weren't forthcoming, he finished for him. "Cyrus Taber. And we've been having some problems in these parts with rustling."

The mention of Taber's name, followed by the word "rustling," opened the flood gates. "Hey now, I ain't rustlin' no beef, Mister Taber," the man said. He shook his head vehemently. "No sir. See, there's this here man in Williams. He buys a beef now and again from Mister Averill. Needs the beef to feed his men. I'm just here to fetch the meat."

Taber's mind clicked like an abacus. He raised the rifle and laid the barrel across his right shoulder. That simple move took all the threat out of his posture. But the man could not see that the gun was still cocked. "That right? Well, then, we have nothing to worry about, do we?" The man nodded tentatively. "You would have some bill of sale with you, then?"

"Bill of sale?"

"Yes. Something signed by Mister Averill." He nodded toward the steer. "That's Triple S beef."

"Well, no, I ain't got no bill of sale. 'Course, my boss would. He does the buyin'."

"Ah, of course. No reason for you to have one if he does. Foolish of me." Taber leaned forward slightly. He was feeling chilled, but the hunt was on and he was in no mood to cut it short. "I never caught your name, sir."

"Webster. My friends call me O. B."

"You work in Williams, then?"

"Yup. Me and the missus."

"And you work for who, Mister Webster?"

The man's face went blank. Taber smiled encouragingly. "Ah, I work for . . . ah . . ."

"Yes?"

"I work for Bert Schmidt," Webster said quickly. "Yup, I work for Bert Schmidt."

"Never had the pleasure of meeting the gentleman."

"Oh," Webster said, waving the hand that still held the knife. "He's just about the biggest logger in these parts. Runs the mill at Williams. Has his own railroad . . . why, you ought to see the pile of sawlogs he's got there on that mountain."

"Sounds like an important man, Mister Schmidt does. He purchases beef from Mister Averill, then, to feed his lumberjacks?"

"That he does." Webster touched a toe to the steer as if for emphasis.

"Well, Mister Webster, I see no reason to keep a man from his work in weather like this. You go about your business."

O. B. Webster's relief was so palpable that Taber grinned. Webster was not bright enough to see that the grin brought no light to the range detective's eyes. His gaze remained as cold and noncommittal as the first moment he had skidded his horse to a stop beside the steer. Taber nodded and moved the palomino toward the trees. He rode no more than two dozen feet before pulling the horse to a halt. He dismounted and dropped the reins, letting them hang free. The palomino made no move to wander off. With the rifle butt resting on the ground, Taber crouched on his haunches. Webster watched him, perplexed. Taber gestured at the steer, as if to encourage Webster to continue with his butchering.

"What you aim to do?" Webster asked. He held the knife uncertainly.

"I aim to sit here until you finish your business with that steer," Taber said quietly. "And then, I figure you and me will take a little ride to Mister Averill's place and have a little chat."

"Now see here," Webster began, still feeling the remains of the initial flush of confidence. "I told you I come by this beef rightful."

"And so you did, Mister Webster, and I would certainly be the last one to doubt your word. But in my business, a man needs to be watchful. You finish up, then we'll just have our little talk with Sam Averill. Then I'm sure you'll be on your way."

"But it's more'n ten miles down there."

"It is that. So, I would suggest you be about your work, Mister Webster. I know Sam Averill and Mister Schmidt will both be unhappy with me, but I do what I'm paid to do."

Webster was loath to put knife to carcass, and he hesitated. Taber sat back on his rump. He moved the rifle slightly so that its muzzle once again pointed in Webster's direction.

"Finish with the beef," he said flatly. Webster began cutting. His nerves were ragged and he did a miserable, dirty job, probably ruining more meat than he saved. More than once, he glanced toward his horse. Taber made note of that, remembering the man's rifle in the saddle boot. When it was clear Webster had the quarter of beef nearly separated, Taber rose and sauntered over to the man's horse. He pulled the rifle from the scabbard. It was an old single shot of buffalo hunter's caliber. It was not loaded, and Taber let it slide back into the rawhide scabbard.

He turned and stood watching Webster. In another ten minutes, the man had wrapped the bloody quarter in an old, dirty piece of burlap. He struggled with it, arranging the bundle on the ground. Finally, he stood up and wiped his hands on his trousers.

"I guess that's it," he announced. "I'll just fetch my horse and we'll be on our way." He didn't sound convinced.

"You only take one quarter?"

"That's all Mister Schmidt wanted."

Taber clicked his tongue. "Such a waste, Mister Webster. Take it all."

"But that's all that . . ."

"I heard what you said." He shifted the rifle. "You will take all the beef your horse can carry, Mister Webster."

"But . . ."

"You will take the beef, sir. All of it. That's what you came for. We will have no waste." He smiled faintly. "It's going to be a long winter. You may need every ounce of that beef."

"I ain't got no more burlap."

"Then you will carry it unwrapped. There are so few flies this time of year, it hardly matters."

If Webster wished to argue, he evidently thought better of it. He was taller, heavier, and no doubt stronger than Cyrus Taber but he was not a fighter by nature, and Taber's authority made anything but compliance impossible. He went back to work as the detective watched patiently. After much struggling, grunting, and sweating, and after much urging from Taber and his rifle, four sections of beef carcass hung from Webster's horse. Had the steer been a large one, the horse would have staggered under the weight.

"Now, I think we can go talk to Mister Averill," Taber said with satisfaction. Both men mounted, one somewhat more eager than the other.

"I ain't never going to make it home before dark," Webster mumbled. He glanced up at the dark sky. Taber said nothing, and felt no pity. For the next three hours, he rode behind O. B. Webster and watched the hunks of beef bounce against the sides of the horse. And he watched Webster cast fleeting glances back at him, and from side to side, as if some avenue of escape would present itself. The prairie was open and, as far as O. B. Webster was concerned, empty. Taber knew there would be no escape for the man, and he was thoroughly pleased with himself.

III

"TABER, come inside a minute." Sam Averill took Taber by the elbow and at the same time turned toward his ranch foreman. "Tom, watch this one. Make sure he doesn't go anywhere."

Averill and Taber walked into the low, dark sod ranch house, leaving Tom Burke to keep the cringing, terrified O. B. Webster company. Webster still sat astride his horse, the beef hanging heavily. With his shoulders slumped and shivering from the growing cold and wind, he was a miserable sight. Tom Burke, on the other hand, seemed immune to the cold. He stood casually on the front porch, leaning against the small hitching post. His revolver was clear of his heavy coat. Ignoring the wind that tugged at the edges of his chaps, he patiently rolled a cigarette. He did not look at Webster. He had no sympathy for the shivering wreck who sat in the saddle.

Sam Averill followed his range detective inside and closed the door against the weather. Averill was pushing fifty, but age had no hold on him—no hold that he allowed to show. He ignored fashion. His face was clean-shaven and ruddy in complexion. His even features were marred only by a ragged scar that ran from his left cheekbone to the corner of his mouth, put there years before when a colt had lashed out and a hoof split open Averill's face to the bone.

The rancher put his hands on his hips and took a deep breath, drawing himself to his full five feet, six inches.

"I admire the way you do your job, Taber," he said. "Shows a lot of patience. You use your head. I appreciate that." Taber nodded but said nothing. "This Webster's just a two-bit

21

ne'er-do-well. Hell, I've seen him around Williams myself. He does odd jobs here and there. Even approached me once, looking for seasonal work. He's no good on a horse, too damned clumsy for much else." Averill smiled faintly and shook his head. "Except rustling, it seems. You care for a brandy?"

Taber nodded again, and Averill walked across the room to fetch the bottle and two glasses. "You know, if I remember right, Webster had himself a woman in town. Don't think he has any young ones." He poured, then handed one of the glasses to Taber. "Not that it matters a hill of beans. Still, I hesitate to string him up. You know why?"

"Schmidt?"

"That's right. If what Webster says is true, if he really is working for Bert Schmidt, maybe we can turn some kind of deal."

"Webster doesn't have much to lose."

"Indeed he doesn't." Averill walked over to one of the windows and looked out. He sipped the brandy. "He's sitting out there right now, knowing he's a dead man." Averill turned and looked at Taber. "Not exactly an enviable position. But, if Webster is working alone, he hangs. That's it. But maybe you're onto something bigger, Taber. I've known Bert Schmidt for years . . . not well, mind you, but well enough that I find what Webster says hard to swallow. But," and he shrugged, "you never know about a man. I can't see a man like Webster being quick enough on his feet to come up with a story like his, unless there's some truth in it. Bert Schmidt is not buying beef from me, we know that much. But he has a good number of men on that mountain of his. Lots of mouths to feed. The gossip has it that he feeds them well, too. He's a businessman. Maybe this is some hare-brained scheme of his to cut costs." Averill laughed dryly. "If that's the case, Schmidt's going to hang himself."

"That's interesting," the range detective said quietly, and drained his glass. "That's interesting. Shouldn't be hard to find out if Webster is telling the truth, or if he's just making up some cock-and-bull story to save his own skin."

"The problem is believing what he has to say. If he is lying to protect himself, we'll find out soon enough. Then he'll hang. He has to know that. If he tells us what we need to know, then . . ."

"Then?"

"I'll leave that up to your best judgment." Averill looked shrewdly at Taber. "I don't like hanging for the sake of hanging," he said. "Use your own judgment."

"I'll take care of things," Taber said and turned toward the door.

"One more thing . . . if Schmidt is taking beef—whether just for his own crews or as part of some bigger rustling operation—and you catch him, there's five hundred dollars in it for you. That's on top of the two hundred for him." Averill nodded in the direction of the door. Taber smiled.

"Fair enough," he said. He pulled his hat down tighter and walked out of the house. Sam Averill closed the door behind the detective and stood quietly, looking down at his empty glass. The rancher did not know Bert Schmidt well, but he knew him well enough to feel uneasy. He shook his head in disgust. "Goddamned fool thing to do," he muttered. "The man's got a thousand square miles of mountain. Seems he could afford to run a hundred head of his own, instead of rustling mine."

Averill wanted to go back outside. He had a hundred chores that needed his attention. Instead, he poured himself another drink, took off his coat, and settled down in a chair to wait for Taber and his catch to be gone from the ranch. He had no stomach for setting eyes on O. B. Webster again.

All but one quarter of the butchered steer stayed at the Averill ranch. Cyrus Taber pushed Webster hard on the return trip to Williams and, even without sparing the horses, it was fully dark before the two men rode the weary mounts

into the mountain village. A score of coal-oil lanterns flick-
ered through glass and oilskin windows. Taber pulled his
palomino to a slow walk.

"You remember what I said," he murmured softly. The
frightened and chilled man nodded immediately. "You try to
run and you won't be safe, no matter where you go. Remember that. And if you run, you'll be leaving your woman
behind." Taber reined in to a halt, and Webster, loath to
spend a second longer in the cold than need be, nevertheless
did the same. Taber leaned forward in the saddle. "You just
go about your business and forget I'm even here. You do
what you would normally do."

"R . . . r . . . right," Webster said, teeth chattering. The wind
had picked up its tempo. Not far from where the two men
sat, a double-trunked pine groaned as it swayed, limbs lash-
ing back and forth. Clouds scudded in from the norhtwest to
hide the stars and threaten the peaks that guarded Williams.
Webster tugged at his coat and glanced furtively at Taber.
The deadly calm of the man was more unnerving than any
storm in any weather, Webster thought, but not as frighten-
ing as what he had to do to save his own life.

"I . . . I need to go home. I never go out . . . I never go up
to Schmidt's until late at night," Webster stammered. Taber
nodded slightly.

"You do that."

"Wh . . . what about you?"

"Don't worry about me, Mister Webster," Taber said quietly. He glanced down the street ahead of them but the
darkness was so intense that all he could see were the dots of
light from scattered buildings. It was as if every shape, every
silhouette, had been erased by the night. He turned and
looked at the dark lump that was Webster. "You go about
your business." Webster needed no more urging. He kicked
his horse and Taber heard the clopping of hooves as the
animal moved up the rough lane between the log buildings.
Occasionally, horse and rider cast a shadow briefly as they

passed a lighted window. Using that as his only reference, Taber urged his palomino forward, following Webster through the village.

They almost had passed entirely through the village and had started up the incline that was the haunch of William's Peak when Webster angled off from the lane toward a cluster of pines and a small, log cabin. Taber stopped his horse immediately. The walls of the cabin were no more than six feet high and the roof was steeply pitched. Taber held his mount perfectly still as he watched Webster dismount and enter the cabin. Yellow light streamed out briefly as the door opened and, for an instant, Taber caught a glimpse of a woman. Then the door closed. The range detective rode forward until he passed under a broom of low hanging pine boughs, then he too dismounted. He glanced up at the sky and pulled his coat tighter against his neck, then turned his attention back to the cabin. His feet began to tingle from the cold and after a moment he reached out, found the large, rough trunk of the nearest pine, and slid down to sit at its base. He pulled his legs up tight against his chest and sat quietly, arms crossed over his knees. He held the reins of his horse in one gloved hand, took a deep breath, and waited. It would have been so much more comfortable to go inside Webster's home, perhaps even to eat dinner with the man and his wife. But Taber wanted no part of that. He did not want to risk being seen with Webster before his work was done. He certainly had no wish to sup with a man he might have to hang.

Bert Schmidt threw another bucket of pine knots into the stove and clanged the door shut. Even inside his snug cabin, he could hear the wind outside and shivered involuntarily. It was at times like this, with the weather turning sour and the ache of a long, hard day in his bones, that Schmidt thought, somewhat wistfully, that a wife would be a fine thing to come home to. Normally, being alone was something Schmidt preferred. He enjoyed his own company. But on nights when the wind howled down from Williams Peak, when the darkness of autumn nights swept through the timber, the loneliness crept in. It hadn't always been that way, but it was that way now, and once in a while, regret crept into Bert Schmidt's life.

He shrugged off the thought, pulled his rocking chair close to the stove, hooked a short log over for a foot rest, adjusted the lantern and picked up the thick book. The new yarn by the Mississippi writer took his mind off things. He saw the raft moving gently along with the thick, muddy water of the great river and forgot about the scream of the steam saw, the heavy thudding of saw logs cant-hooked into the carriage, the shouts and curses of the men, the weather outside. So engrossed was he in the tale of the boy and the black man that he didn't hear the faint, tentative knock on his door. Eventually he looked up, frowned, and lay the book down. When he opened the door, he half expected his mill foreman to be standing there with news of another problem. Jean-Paul Gingras spent long hours at the mill, working well beyond quitting time to maintain the machinery for the next day's work. But the man standing in front of Schmidt's door was not Gingras. He was holding a heavy burlap bundle by one corner while the bulk of the weight rested on the ground.

The light was so poor that Schmidt did not recognize O. B. Webster. The brim of the man's hat shadowed his face from the cabin light, and he stood well away from the doorway. Something was wrong, Schmidt sensed immediately. The man was nervous and shifted from foot to foot. As Schmidt opened the door, the man glanced over his shoulder in the direction of the trees down the hill.

"Yes?" Schmidt said. Webster didn't reply. He looked off into the darkness again. Schmidt saw nothing except the faint outlines of the wind-whipped limbs of the nearest pine.

"If you have business with me, come inside. All the heat's going out this door."

Webster jerked his head back and looked at Schmidt. "I got your beef," he said loudly, louder than was necessary. The sound carried over the moaning wind.

"You what?"

The man looked down and pulled at the burlap. "I got the side of beef you wanted," he repeated. Schmidt frowned and looked puzzled.

"Who the hell are you? And what's this about beef? Anyone walking around the mountain on a night like this peddling beef is plumb crazy. You must take me for someone else. Goodnight to you, sir." Schmidt started to close the door, but the man stepped forward quickly, pulling at the bundle.

"You got to take it," he shouted. His voice cracked with something that to Schmidt sounded mighty close to fear. "Look here," the man continued. Webster spoke like a drunk who thought his audience deaf. He bent down and fumbled with the burlap. A portion fell away and Schmidt saw the dark shadow of the contents. If it was beef, he had to take the man's word for it. He had no more interest in it than that.

"I don't know what your game is, mister, but you'd best be on your way," Schmidt said quietly. He moved the door again and started to step back. The chill was creeping through his heavy shirt and he was irritated. To his astonishment, Webster straightened up and nodded vehemently.

"That's what you said," he announced loudly. "This is your beef. You ordered it and now I want my money. I done my part, now you owe me."

At that point, a movement caught Schmidt's eye. He squinted into the dark and saw the motion again. "What the hell is going on?" he muttered. The movement materialized into another man, a man making his way up toward Schmidt's cabin. When the figure was a dozen yards away,

Schmidt could see that he was carrying what had to be a rifle. Without conscious thought, Schmidt's body weight transferred to the balls of his feet and his hand on the door tensed. Other than that, he made no move. Webster noticed Schmidt's stance and turned to face the man. His back was very nearly square to Schmidt and slightly to one side of the door. In that instant, from the corner of his eye, Schmidt saw the back of the man's coat belch outwards. Simultaneously a gun roared further down the hill from the cover of the timber. Webster slammed backwards and thudded heavily into the wall. His breath exploded out with a loud gasp. The man approaching dove off to one side and Schmidt jerked back.

"Christ, not me," Schmidt heard the wounded man murmur. With his hands holding his belly, Webster began to slide down the wall. His mouth was open in astonishment. Schmidt instinctively crouched and sidestepped away from the open door. He thought first of his own rifle across the cabin, leaning in a corner. But before he could move, another shot rang out and this time Schmidt heard the loud whack of the slug's impact. Webster jerked upright. His hands fluttered up to the center of his coat and he turned slowly toward the door. If there was any expression on his face at all, it was complete bewilderment. His eyes met Schmidt's for a heartbeat, then lost focus. He fell forward toward Schmidt. His head cracked the door jamb and he hit the floor with a thump, his upper body inside the cabin. Webster's body tensed and one hand clawed at the wood of the floor. A faint, high-pitched sigh came from somewhere deep inside him, and then he was still.

Schmidt charged across the cabin and grabbed the rifle. He turned and then stopped short. Standing just inside his cabin's doorway, protected by the bulk of the log walls, was a slender, short man wearing a heavy sheepskin coat. He was leaning slightly forward, squinting off into the darkness. He held a rifle and his finger rested on the trigger.

"I think they've gone," the man said. He did not turn to acknowledge Schmidt's presence. They both heard brush crashing in the distance, and the man nodded. "They're going on down the hill." Schmidt advanced across the cabin, rifle in hand.

"Just who the hell are you?" he snapped, and the man turned. He was a stranger. Schmidt was about to repeat the question when Webster drew one leg slowly up and sighed again. Schmidt crossed quickly to him, leaned the rifle against the wall, and knelt down. "Close that damned door," he said. He gripped the wounded man's coat and pulled him inside. As he rolled Webster over on his back, the stranger closed the door. In the ragged coat, the bullet holes were scarcely noticeable. By the time Schmidt had torn open the coat and the sodden shirt and woolen long johns, the man was dead. The wounds were dead center, one near the belt line and the other a hand's spread higher.

"He's dead," Schmidt said. He grimaced and pulled the clothing back together. "Maybe you'd better explain what the hell is going on." He pushed himself to his feet.

"I thought I'd get the answers from you, Mister Schmidt." The man's voice was soft and Schmidt turned to face him. The logger found himself staring into the dark muzzle of the man's rifle.

IV

BERT Schmidt could do little about unexpected, long-range rifle shots that thundered from the dark protection of timber during the night. But a rifle thrust in his face was another matter. Cyrus Taber was used to seeing fear and hesitation in men's eyes. Before his gloved finger even could squeeze the trigger of the cocked Winchester, the barrel of the .44 was smashed aside.

Schmidt moved in fast. Although he was not particularly tall, he weighed nearly two hundred pounds, not much of which was fat. His hands, gnarled from a lifetime of heavy labor, were hard as boards. He grabbed Taber by the collar of his coat and spun him viciously around in a circle, using the momentum to slam the man up against a wall, face first. Taber was so surprised that he had no time to defend himself. Schmidt spun him back and drove a knee hard into the man's groin. Taber doubled over, lips compressed tightly against the pain. Even in agony, the range detective sought to bring the rifle up. It was a feeble reaction at best and a foolish one. Schmidt smacked Taber backhanded so hard that the man's head snapped back and banged dully into the wall. Taber released the rifle and crumpled against the logs.

"I don't know who you are, mister," Schmidt said, breathing heavily with rage, "but you'd better crawl your ass out of this cabin and get off my property." He grabbed the rifle from where it lay on the floor and held it like a club, his fists clenched tightly around the barrel. His rage was so intense that he didn't remember to check whether the rifle was cocked. With a savage swing, he smashed it down against the thick boards of the floor splintering the stock. The rifle was only months old and its trigger sear was clean and sharp. It remained cocked, a live cartridge in the chamber. As Taber watched in disbelief, Schmidt flung open the door and hurled the broken rifle far into the night. The logger stood in the doorway and glared down at Taber. "Now, get out." Taber mumbled something but the stabbing pain at both ends of his body made coherent thought all but impossible. "You want help?" Schmidt snarled. He stepped toward the prostrate man, intending to grab Taber and hurl him out the door after the broken rifle. Taber held up a hand.

"Wait," he whispered. "For God's sakes . . ."

"There's nothing I need to discuss with the likes of you," Schmidt said. He still held open the door, ignorant of the cold that whistled into the cabin.

"What about him?" Taber managed. He nodded toward the corpse that was still bleeding on the floor.

"What about him?" Schmidt was still breathing heavily, but he reached behind himself and closed the door. Taber felt a surge of relief. "I don't know who he was, or who killed him, or even why, for God's sakes," Schmidt said. "He's dead, and you stick a goddamned gun in my face."

"He was a rustler," Taber said, lurching painfully to a sitting position. Schmidt was standing still and listening, so Taber continued, trying to put the pain in his crotch and in his head out of mind. "He said you hired him."

Schmidt put his hands on his hips and stared at the man. "God almighty, you are a cocky little son of a bitch. I don't know that man from Adam. You run in here, stick a goddamned rifle in my face, and now you accuse me of rustling cattle! I ought to throw you out that door." He took a threatening step forward.

"Wait . . . you don't know who that is?"

"I already said as much."

"His name's O. B. Webster. He lives right here in the village."

Schmidt turned and stared at the corpse. For the first time, the face looked a little familiar. He looked back at Taber. "So do a hundred other people I don't know, or care to know. Just who the hell are you?"

Taber grimaced and tried to sit straighter. "You are a quick man with your hands, Mister Schmidt." He managed a grim smile. "Name's Taber. I work for Sam Averill."

"Averill hires the likes of you? I thought better of him."

"There's been rustling."

"So you say. You caught him at it?" Schmidt indicated Webster's remains with a brief nod.

"I did. South of here, near the timberline." Taber finally freed a hand from his groin and tenderly felt the side of his face. "He said you hired him to rustle cattle. So you could feed your men."

Schmidt laughed shortly. "That's the goddamnedest thing I ever heard. I buy beef for my men and I buy potatoes, and flour, and you name it. I got the goddamned best cooks this side of the Canadian border. I could buy out half of Sam Averill's herd if I wanted. Hell, the whole herd. Why in hell would I bother ferreting around at night, trying to skin one mangy steer at a time?"

"I thought maybe you could tell me that."

"You don't give up, do you? I've spent all the time talking to you that I'm about to. Get out. And take this Webster with you. You want to find answers, you find out who put two holes in him."

"Maybe whoever it was, was aiming for you."

"Bullshit."

Taber struggled to his feet, but found it impossible to stand erect. He made an effort anyway, his pride hurting. "You sound mighty sure of yourself."

"You don't miss twice by putting the bullets through another man's guts," Schmidt said. "You tell Sam Averill I want to see him." Schmidt stabbed an index finger into Taber's chest so hard the detective winced. "You tell him I want him at my mill tomorrow. If he doesn't show, by God I'll ride down to the Triple S myself." Taber could see Schmidt was working himself into another fury, so the detective struggled toward the door. The logger caught Taber by the arm. "And the next time you decide to come pay me a nighttime visit, you best yell out well ahead. Otherwise, I'll blow your god-damned head clean off your sneaky shoulders. Maybe you get your chuckles out of sticking rifles in folks' faces, but by God, you don't do that to me." Schmidt opened the door again, but blocked the detective's way. "I said take Webster with you. And his beef."

"I can't do that."

"By God you will do it."

"What am I supposed to do with him?" Taber's cheeks flushed with anger.

"I really don't care, Taber. I'm sure a resourceful man like you will think of something." There was no point in arguing, Taber could see.

"I'm sure we'll meet again," he said. He bent down and grabbed Webster under the arms.

"You just keep your snot-nosed threats to yourself, and remember what I said about Averill. I don't care if you have to ride all goddamned night." He watched Taber drag the corpse out the door. The body smeared through the puddle of thick blood that had seeped from the back of Webster's coat. Taber was making slow progress with the corpse, and Schmidt added to his burden by tossing the haunch of beef at him. The bundle hit with enough force to jar Taber's grip loose, and he glared venomously at Schmidt. "And get that off my property," Schmidt spat, stepping back inside and slamming the door shut.

Taber stood still for a moment, silently cursing. In all his thirty-six years, he had been struck by other men only twice. He had never been humiliated. He looked back up the hill at Bert Schmidt's door as he renewed his grip on the corpse and the bundle of beef. "We'll see, mister high and mighty," he breathed. "We'll see."

V

THROUGHOUT the night, Bert Schmidt slept fitfully. Hours after Taber had left with the corpse, after he had cleaned up the mess on the floor, Schmidt's anger cooled enough for him to know he had handled things badly. He knew he had made an enemy of the range detective, but the man had had no cause to push the rifle in his face. He lay in bed and thought about Webster—who he might have been, why he had brought his own troubles to Schmidt's doorstep. But finally, Schmidt slept. When he awoke, his toes and nose told him the house was colder than it should be. He curled tightly, forestalling the inevitable. Across the room from his cot, the potbellied stove stood black and cold, waiting. The pine knots and mill scraps he fed the stove produced fierce heat, but they didn't hold overnight. Maybe Mike Buchanan's idea of coal wasn't such a bad one, he thought.

He lifted his head and looked through the dim morning light toward the door. The smudge was still evident on the floor. Whoever Webster had been, it was someone else's business. That was all there was to it. In his rage the night before, he had demanded that Sam Averill ride nearly thirty miles to see him. But in the cold of that morning, Bert Schmidt didn't really care whether Averill showed or not.

The logger raised his head from under the blankets and fumbled for the box of matches. The house was beginning to gather the dawn light, and Schmidt's inner clock told him it was time. He struck a match and held it to the wick of the lantern near his bed. By the time the wick flared and he had the chimney replaced, his arms were covered with goose bumps. He looked at his pocket watch, then lay back down, snuggling under the blankets. Outside, he could hear the moan of the wind. Once, he heard the rattle of something against the window when a gust shook the trees near the cabin.

He listened, then tensed. "One, two, three," he said aloud, and threw the covers off. He grabbed the box of matches, walked quickly to the stove, and threw the door open. A coal or two of pine still smoldered deep inside. He reached into the wood box and took a fistfull of tinder. That and a burning match went into the stove, followed by kindling. The tinder caught. He thrust in more kindling and clanged the door shut. He shot open the lower grate and twisted open the chimney damper. While he waited for the roaring in the stove to grow, Schmidt dressed, ending the ritual by sitting in the rocking chair to lace up his heavy boots. He rose and walked to the window. As he peered out, he grinned widely.

"Well, it's about time," he said happily. Four inches of snow covered the ground and more was slanting down through the pines near the cabin. The wind racked the deep shadows of the timber, the hiss of the storm music to Schmidt's ears.

He crossed to the window beside the front door. On the frame, just outside the glass, was a thermometer Schmidt had purchased mail-order four winters before. He squinted through a spider web of frost but couldn't read the scale. He fetched the lantern and held it up, then whistled. The mercury sat at zero degrees. He tapped on the window glass as if that might jar the mercury up the scale. "Son of a gun," he muttered. "This is November, not February. No damned wonder it's cold in here." He put the lantern down and fed the stove a scuttle full of pine knots. "Damned wash water's probably froze," he mumbled. It wasn't, but it hadn't missed by much. Schmidt drew off a pot of water from the small cistern for coffee, threw in a handful of grounds, and brought the pot to the stove. While the coffee was heating, he washed and looked in the mirror. More gray was creeping into his hair each day, but that didn't concern him. Schmidt's father had been bald as an egg from age thirty-five on but Schmidt had passed that mark seven years before. His hair was still all there, a dark, salt-and-pepper thatch that he combed sideways with his fingers. His full beard was complemented by shaggy eyebrows that hung over eyes the color of obsidian. When the coffee was ready, Schmidt took it off the stove and poured a cup, not noticing that it was more grounds than water. After that, he sat down by the stove to begin the next part of his morning ritual. In a heavy bound diary, he meticulously entered the events of the day before. The entry for November 16, 1886, took more time than usual. He also briefly noted what he hoped to accomplish that day, November 17, 1886. Bert Schmidt had been writing his notes faithfully for nearly thirty-five years. His father had done the same, and his grandfather, and probably even his great-grandfather before that. As he wrote his comments on the weather, he wondered who would keep and read the diaries, his included, after his death. He put the volume back on the shelf to one side of the stove, fed the potbellied stove, and closed down the dampers.

Schmidt's cabin sat deep in the timber above Williams, a hundred yards from his sawmill. By the time he set out through the driving snow that morning, a reluctant dawn was giving some character to the country. There was enough light to see the great mushroom of the chip burner behind the mill. Today, the burner would fire up, sending its plumes of rich, fragrant smoke over the valley and keeping the sawmill from burying itself under mounds of wood scraps.

More important, Schmidt knew Phillip Scott would be eager to make a run with the locomotive. Scott loved that engine as much as he hated working in the mill when the locomotive was idle. Schmidt was eager to start hauling too, for ricks of sawn timber and boards and mining trusses had risen high in the yard. The most impatient customers had delivery by freight wagon, but that took time. Now, the four flatcars were loaded and waiting. The snow meant they would move, heading south on the narrow-gauge to the main line siding thirty-five miles down Sutton Creek.

Schmidt headed not to the mill that morning but to the kitchen. He scuffed his way through the snow with delight, head cocked against the wind. The log building's steeply pitched roof capped a structure forty feet long and twenty-six wide. Inside were rough-hewn tables and benches and, at one end, a large stove. Schmidt could see the smoke rolling out of the chimney whipped instantly away by the wind. The other end of the lodge was the domain of two men whom no logger working for Schmidt would ever cross. Smoke issued from a chimney at that end of the hall as well, and Schmidt quickened his pace.

He stepped inside and slammed the door behind him, then stamped his feet and pulled off his gloves. The aroma from the kitchen filled his nostrils. In the large kitchen at the end of the chowhall worked Charles D'Arlene and Pierre Juteau. The fragrance of their handiwork began at four each morning. Bert Schmidt knew what good food meant to hard working men and he met his responsibility without regard to cost. Schmidt's deal with his men, whether loggers, sawyers, or common mill hands, was simple. If they wanted lodging, they could build log cabins near the mill, using cull logs at no charge. Perhaps thirty small cabins dotted the hillsides and meadows, most simple, some lavish. Board cost five dollars a week. The loggers ate breakfast in the chowhall and by the time they were finished, their lunches were packed and ready. Supper was served promptly at seven. Loggers with families usually took care of their own food.

In the chowhall that morning were a dozen mill hands. The loggers had already left for the woods in order to be on the job by six-thirty. Schmidt was greeted casually as he crossed to the kitchen and stood in front of the counter. Years before, Juteau had rigged a horizontal swinging door that swung down to close off the kitchen from the rest of the chowhall. When the kitchen was closed, no one even dared knock. The cook was temperamental and fast with a cleaver. As Schmidt approached, Juteau slapped down a metal cup and filled it with coffee.

"You almost missed," he said shortly to Schmidt. "The eggs are gone."

"Then I'll take whatever's left," Schmidt said, and matched Juteau's snarl with a frown. The Canadian had appointed himself sergeant-at-arms for the chowhall, and he greeted tardiness with disgust. He was short and stocky and prone to wilt late arrivals with a black-eyed glare—an especially effective tactic since besides having a bulldog disposition, Juteau was also one of the ugliest men ever placed on earth. Virtually everything was wrong with his face—forehead too low, eyes closely set, jaw too large, nose misshapen. Juteau's boss, Charles D'Arlene, was content to let Juteau deal with the hungry. Charles D'Arlene rarely spoke. He occasionally consulted with Juteau, in French, but otherwise kept to himself, running the kitchen in his own way.

In seconds, Schmidt was handed a metal plate heaped with potatoes, a small beefsteak, and three flapjacks that were dripping with melted butter.

"That's all there is," Juteau announced righteously. To him, his employer's portion amounted to almost a starvation diet. He softened momentarily. "You want some pie?"

"What kind?"

Juteau shrugged. "The only left is blueberry." His lilting accent emphasized the last syllable of the name.

"Yeah, gimme some of that. Don't want to starve on a day like this." Juteau put the pie on top of the potatoes. "Thanks," Schmidt said wryly. He sat down beside a large, square-faced man at the end of a table. The man pointed a fork at the pie.

"Interesting gravy," he said sagely.

"It all ends up in the same place," Schmidt muttered as he grinned at his foreman. Jean-Paul Gingras pushed away his plate and cradled his coffee cup in his large hands. It was almost hot in the chowhall. Gingras's sleeves were rolled tightly over his beefy forearms. "I want the engine to run today. Thank God for this storm," Schmidt said.

"That is the first thing Phillip said this morning," Gingras replied.

"Might have guessed as much. By the way, there's coal down at the Sutton siding. Belongs to Mike Buchanan. We need to start bringing that up on return trips. Remember to tell Scott to take the boxcar."

"He knows. He told me so this morning."

"Just so he doesn't forget. Buchanan's been yelping about that coal for weeks. He'll have our ass if we put him off now."

Gingras nodded. "So we start the mill run for Brown today."

"I wonder if he's still going to build his whorehouse?" Schmidt mused.

Gingras grinned.

Schmidt pushed his empty plate away. "Pie was the best part of breakfast," he said, turning to Gingras. "You hear the shooting last night?"

"Shooting? No." Gingras lived down in the village with his wife and two children, and Schmidt was more than curious to know whether any talk had already begun.

Schmidt briefly told Gingras his story, the Frenchman's forehead wrinkling in disbelief. "Sacré bleu," Gingras murmured when Schmidt had finished. "You do not remember this Webster? I do. He worked for us two years ago. For only a month, as I remember, maybe two at the most."

"Nope. What happened? Why'd he quit?"

Gingras shrugged. "He did not like work. He did not like horses, was clumsy with tools. He worked in the mill for maybe one week. That Webster was sent to me from the timber because Stan Chester was disgusted with his work. I fired him after a week. But who shot him? You never saw?"

"No. Came out of the trees. Maybe fifty yards away."

The Frenchman rubbed the stubble on his chin. "Why do you suppose he picked on you, eh? Maybe your name just came to mind. Maybe he thought you would be in the market."

"And walk all the way up the mountain in the dark? Doesn't make sense."

"And the range detective, this Taber, he followed him up?"

"Looked that way. The way Webster was looking over his shoulder, he must have expected somebody. He didn't try to run when he saw Taber. And the way he talked . . . maybe he had something cooking with Taber. He sure wasn't shouting for my benefit." Schmidt took a last drink of the strong coffee. "At any rate, I told Taber to send his boss up here today." He glanced out one of the windows. "I don't much expect him to get here though." He frowned. "This Webster have a family?"

"A wife. Do you suppose Taber took the body to her?"

Schmidt sighed. "Damned if I know. He's going to have to settle it up with her somehow. He knows I had nothing to do with the shooting." He fiddled with his cup. "I keep telling myself it's none of my business. But when a man dies on your doorstep, it kind of becomes your business, doesn't it?"

Gingras nodded slowly. "Especially when he dies with your name on his lips."

"That's not exactly what happened, Jean-Paul. I tell you, when someone gets killed in the mill, or out in the timber, you know what to do. It's over and settled. But something like this . . ." Schmidt shook his head. "Maybe Williams needs some law, Jean-Paul. It's been a quiet little town up to now." He glanced at Gingras. "These Websters have any children?"

"I knew them only a little, mon ami. I would recognize her if I saw her, that is all. I do not think there were any children."

"Something needs to be done for the woman." Schmidt nodded toward the window, whose panes were thick with frost. "Winter is finally coming on." He looked at Gingras.

The Frenchman's face was sober. "Woman marries a no-good like Webster, her life's bound to be one hardship after another," he said.

The wrinkles around Gingras's eyes deepened and a trace of a smile crossed his face. "You think she is your concern, eh?"

"Hell, more like Sam Averill's concern. He pays Taber. They're mixed up in this somehow."

"As you are. Maybe Marshall Markham should be told."

"Jim Markham's honest but he's a lousy lawman. Besides, he has no authority in Williams," Schmidt said.

"Nor does anyone else."

Schmidt gave a nod and added, "It'd take us nine years to get a U.S. marshall to wander over here. I guess we'll just see how things resolve themselves." He gathered his cup and plate and stood up. "I don't think Taber will be back."

"If I were you, my friend, I would not wait too long." Gingras stood up, towering over Schmidt by nearly six inches. He was a great, wide hulk of a man. "I would not wait for things to, ah, as you suggest, resolve themselves. They may resolve the wrong way."

VI

BY midmorning, it was apparent that the storm was not just a late autumn snow flurry, for nearly six inches had been hurled against the flank of Williams Peak by the northwest wind. The wind heaped the fine pellets under the trees, massing drifts against the trunks, plastering the snow onto the bark. Each tree on the mountain bore a white stripe up its bole. The snow lashed around the sawmill and sifted through cracks. It seeped under doors and piled around the great ricks of timber. The storm moaned like a banshee, and shivered the snow-laden boughs.

In such weather, the mill was a miserable place to be. The ends of the building gaped open to the elements. The steam boiler powered a whirl of machinery where an inattentive sawyer could lose an arm or his life if his concentration lapsed. That morning, the boiler wasn't creating an island of warmth to cheer the mill hands but a slurry of melting snow and sawdust. The footing near the saws was slick. Ice and packed snow clogged the carriage that drove the logs toward the saw blades. Still, the five-foot circular blades screamed through the timber.

Schmidt left the mill to Gingras. He retreated into his small office where a miniature potbellied stove allowed him to work in his shirtsleeves. He hunched over his desk and read through an order for the mill.

As Bert Schmidt worked that fall morning, the storm that hurled in from the northwest all but choked the village below, the dense, swirling snow clouds keeping the valley in half-light. A solitary figure struggled through the tall pines that stood sentinel between mill and village. From time to time, she stopped, breathing hard from the exertion of her climb and the rage that drove her on.

By the time she had managed half the distance up the hill, her ears, cheeks, and nose were numb. Once, she tumbled headlong into the snow, then resolutely lurched to her feet and plunged on, eyes fixed on the mill. Snow in her coat sleeves formed painful bracelets around her wrists. Her boots were nearly full and the melting ice soaked her feet. She didn't think about those things, though.

At last, the woman reached the level stretch on which the mill stood and began to work her way around to the end of the building. At the corner her way was blocked by the butt ends of nearly a hundred logs. She headed instinctively toward the sounds of machinery.

When she rounded the end of the log pile, she was able to look into the dark interior of the mill where she saw men jostling logs toward the saw carriage. All the motion and activity made her pause. Though he was nearly blinded by wind-whipped snow and wood chips, Jean-Paul Gingras spied the small figure. From a distance, she looked like a miniature ghost lost in the storm. Assuming it was a child belonging to one of the mill hands, Gingras waved her away from the machinery. She didn't move. Impatient with the interruption, Gingras motioned for one of his workers to take his post near the cut-off saw. The big Frenchman carefully made his way down the length of the carriage to the far wall. Between the two of them were saw logs lined up end to end on the carriage. He beckoned to the figure, summoning her out of the storm. Only when she was a dozen feet away did he realize her true age. She wore no hat, her long hair was full of snow, and she was shivering violently. He stood between her and the machinery and shouted over the din. "What is the matter? Who do you want?" Perhaps an emergency had driven the woman out in the storm to fetch her man home. That puzzled him, since he knew all the men well, and knew their wives. Still, perhaps one of them, one of the unmarried ones, had a girlfriend. He saw her mouth moving, but couldn't hear what she said. He made his way to her, leaned down, and cocked his head. At the same time, as if by instinct, he placed a large hand on one of her thin shoulders. He could feel the woman shake.

"Bert Schmidt," he heard her yell. He looked at her in surprise.

"You want to see Mister Schmidt?" The woman nodded in agitation. She looked vaguely familiar then, but Gingras was more concerned with getting back to work. He'd need luck to get the woman to Schmidt's office without her falling into the saws, Gingras thought. He briefly toyed with the notion of bringing Schmidt out, but the woman looked miserable, and the office was warm and reasonably quiet.

Gingras walked slightly behind the woman, holding her right elbow. She was tense as timber. The woman did not flinch as they passed the headsaws, nor was she bothered by the saws' shower of bark and dust. She moved as if she were under a spell, oblivious to all around her. The mill hands and sawyers glanced at her briefly and quickly turned back to their work.

Schmidt's office door was closed so Gingras reached past the woman to finger the latch. It was at that point, as he pushed the door and the woman's face was illuminated by the lantern in Schmidt's small office, that the Frenchman recognized her. She stepped into the office and Gingras started to close the door. Schmidt stood up, astonished. A woman half destroyed by the storm was the last interruption he expected.

The storm saved Bert Schmidt's life. With deliberation, the woman drew an enormous old revolver from her coat. But the cold had made her movements sluggish and uncoordinated. She raised the gun with both hands. One hand fumbled with the hammer as she tried to cock the weapon. Schmidt was so startled by the muzzle that wavered in his general direction that he stood open-mouthed. With one arm, Gingras slammed the door shut and with the other crashed the woman against a wall. The gun, still uncocked, clattered to the floor. The woman hit the rough wood of the wall and collapsed in a heap on the floor.

Schmidt almost cracked heads with Gingras as the two men rushed to kneel beside the woman. She was incoherent, half from the cold and half from Gingras's blow. She would have been almost pretty but for the ice that matted to her hair and the sobs that contorted her face.

"Who the hell is she?" Schmidt shouted to his foreman.

Gingras patted the woman's shoulder as if that might help heal her troubles. He was already feeling miserable for hitting her. "This, mon ami, is Mrs. Webster." He glanced at Schmidt. "I did not recognize her until I had opened the door. I am sorry."

"Let's get her to the chowhall," Schmidt said. He shifted and felt something sharp under his knee. It was the revolver. He glanced at it quickly before tossing it onto his desk. The weapon was fully loaded and capped.

"Christ," Schmidt muttered. "Take her elbow," he then said to Gingras, and the two men gently pulled the woman to her feet. She hung like a sack of beans. Schmidt wrapped her coat around her shaking body. From his desk, he picked up his own woolen stocking cap and pulled it down over the woman's head, covering her to the eyebrows. The woman allowed herself to be led out of the mill and once more into the teeth of the storm. Gingras and Schmidt hustled her across the lumber yard to the chowhall so fast that the tips of the woman's toes barely touched the snow.

There they met with the smells and warmth that only a working kitchen could produce. "Take her over beside the stove," Schmidt ordered, motioning toward the cherry-red stove at the end of the hall opposite the kitchen. "We got an hour before the men come in for lunch. I want to know why she wants my hide."

VII

CARLOTTA Webster glanced across the plank table at the face she thought she hated but saw only concern in Bert Schmidt's eyes. Her hysteria had subsided and she was confused by the awkwardly compassionate care she had received in the past half hour. From the kitchen came a pot of the strongest coffee she had ever tasted, and a warm towel. The huge mill foreman, Jean-Paul Gingras, dried her hair with the towel as if she was a child who'd been caught in the rain. When he finished, her hair was disheveled but almost dry. With the second cup of coffee and the whiskey that laced it, the shake in her hands had subsided. She held the cup with both hands, afraid to meet the gaze of either man.

She was a pretty woman, Schmidt reflected. He poured himself a cup of the strong brew as well, and waited patiently until Carlotta was ready to speak.

"I will go back to the mill," Gingras said quietly, putting on his coat.

"All right," Schmidt said. Carlotta lifted her head. "Thank you," she said softly. Her voice was husky. "I'm sorry for the trouble I've caused."

"It is nothing," Gingras replied. He shrugged and grinned at Schmidt. "After all, the gun did not go off, did it?" Gingras left, and Schmidt picked up the coffee pot.

"More?"

"No," she said. "No, thank you." She sighed raggedly and stared at the table. "I was wrong, wasn't I?"

"You think I killed your husband but I didn't." Schmidt paused and noticed that the woman was finally looking at him. "I don't know who did."

"Cyrus Taber said you did."

"Then Taber is a liar." He imagined the range detective dragging the corpse of O. B. Webster to the widow's door and then pointing an accusing finger back up the hill. "Tell me what else he told you."

It was still difficult for Carlotta to speak of the incident, and she hastily took another drink to regain control of her nerves.

"Take your time," Schmidt said. "Why don't you tell me what happened from the beginning? Did Taber bring your husband's body to your home last night?" Carlotta nodded, scarcely able to control her tears.

"Someone sent for the parson," she said in a whisper. "I don't know who. He and Milly came and took Ossie to . . ." She stopped speaking and covered her face with her hands.

"Ossie?"

She reached over and took the rough towel Gingras had used, and held it to her face as if she might be sick. "I called him Ossie," she mumbled. She kept her eyes tightly closed. "Most folks called him O. B."

"Your husband was involved somehow in rustling," Schmidt said gently. "Did you know about that?"

Carlotta was a long time answering. She lowered the towel and held it twisted around her hands. "That's what Mister Taber said. I don't believe it. If he was rustling cattle, it's because he was forced to, somehow. Mister Taber said you were paying my husband."

"You believe that?" Schmidt didn't give her time to answer. "If I needed beef, I'd buy it fair and square. Someone was paying your husband, Mrs. Webster. That's the way it seems to me. But it wasn't me. Maybe your husband owed someone money—more than he could pay."

Carlotta managed a trace of a smile. "He owed everyone

money, Mister Schmidt. He just couldn't seem . . . to manage, somehow." She looked up defiantly. "I loved him no less for that. He was . . . he was a good man. He had his faults, but he was good."

Indeed, Schmidt thought grimly. "What made you decide to come up here?"

Carlotta closed her eyes and shook her head. "Mister Taber said you jumped him and . . . and beat him. I saw the marks on his face. He said you had killed my husband, but that the law would never touch you."

"And so you fetched that horse pistol and . . ."

Carlotta nodded. A thought occurred to Schmidt, and he asked, "Did you load that pistol yourself, Mrs. Webster?" She shook her head. "Who did, then?"

"Mister Taber. He said I should have something, being alone."

"Very thoughtful of him."

"What will happen to me now?" Carlotta whispered.

"We'll do our best to get you home without your freezing. You know, in a way, I admire what you did. You're a brave woman, Mrs. Webster." Schmidt smiled. "Foolish, at least just a little, but brave. I'm sorry about your husband. For my part, I intend to find out who is responsible. He'll be brought to justice, I guarantee." He paused. "I have just one more question, and I'd like an honest answer." He looked hard at the woman, and she met his gaze without flinching. "Do you still believe that I had anything to do with your husband's death?"

"I don't believe you killed my husband, no."

"Fine," and Schmidt stood up abruptly. "Let's see about getting you home."

"Mister Schmidt . . ."

"Yes?"

"I came up here to . . . to shoot you. I was so sure. And now, I think you may be the one person in Williams who I can really trust."

"I would hope there are others."

She rose slowly, and carefully folded the towel. "You've done me a kindness I did not deserve."

"We all make mistakes," Schmidt said. "Let's get you home. Wait here a few minutes. I'll have one of the wagons around to the door."

"There's no need of that."

"Need or not, you stay here." Schmidt left the chowhall, went to the stock barn, and made quick work of harnessing one of the Belgians to a small freight wagon. The wind had slackened some, but the snow still stung his face. Only after he had driven the wagon outside did he remember his coat. He made his way to his office, dressed against the weather, and went back to the wagon. The big horse snorted and shook its head to clear its ears of snow. Schmidt drove the wagon up to the chowhall, and then, with the woman aboard, headed down the hill trail to Williams. The Belgian was slow but sure-footed, and Schmidt let the animal set his own pace. Once down the hill, Schmidt pulled the horse and wagon to a stop in front of the woman's cabin. He helped her down and walked her to the front door, both of them holding their heads down against the snow and cold. "I'll let you know what I find out," he said, and left quickly.

Before returning to the mill, he drove into the heart of the village, and pulled up in front of the emporium. Inside, he caught Mike Buchanan's eye and waved him over. The bartender left his customers and walked into the general merchandise section of the store.

Schmidt drew him aside, but Buchanan spoke first. "Say, what's this I hear about you shooting O. B. Webster?" he said with a scowl.

"Don't be an ass, Mike," Schmidt said testily. "Someone shot him . . . but it wasn't me."

"Who did it?"

"I don't know. But I aim to find out. Now listen. This is just between you and me, you understand?"

"Sure," Buchanan nodded, looking puzzled. "What's between us?"

"Mrs. Webster got much of a bill with you?"

Buchanan shrugged. "Few bucks. Going to be hard for her now. Old O. B. didn't leave much, would be my guess. Probably didn't leave a red cent."

"Winter coming on, it's going to be tougher. If she comes in here, just put what she needs on my bill." Schmidt saw Buchanan's surprise. "Look, she needs help. It isn't going to hurt me much. But don't you go blabbing this around."

Buchanan looked a little dubious, but said, "Well, all right. Sure. We'll help her all we can. Come spring, she can figure out what to do. We'll carry her."

"Good."

"Say," and Buchanan laid a hand on Schmidt's arn "You reckon on bringing up my coal?"

"Scott's got the engine running. He'll be taking a load of timber down to the railhead tomorrow, if the storm doesn't get worse. Things go right, he'll bring your coal back on the return trip. You should have it Friday. Maybe Saturday, latest. You have some men set to unload the boxcar, because I got me more timber to load." He grinned. "I guess we both have some impatient customers."

"We'll be ready," Buchanan said, rubbing his hands together in delight. "This winter's going to be a killer, you mark my words. That coal's going to be worth same as gold."

Schmidt smiled wryly. "You may be right after all. I'm going to have to charge you more for the freighting of it, with you making all that money."

Buchanan's face registered mock horror. "Don't do that to me, Bert." He held up his hands, then became serious. "You ain't got any idea about the shooting? Terrible thing."

"No, but I intend to find out, like I say. There's a range detective bent on blaming me for both the murder and the rustling. I don't know what gave him that notion. He needs to be set straight."

"That be Cyrus Taber?"

"The same. Works for Sam Averill."

"I've seen him around town," Buchanan said. He wrinkled his face with distaste. "Slimy little bastard."

"He's going to be more than slimy by the time I get through with him, I promise you that. He was there when Webster got shot. He knows I didn't do it, but he told the widow I did. She came to the mill to put some lead in me."

Buchanan's eyes went wide. "She did that? Damn. She missed, eh?"

"She missed altogether. Gun never went off. We had us a talk afterwards. She's cooled down some."

"If that don't beat all. Well," Buchanan said and thrust his hands in his trouser pockets, "you let me know what I can do to help. We don't need the likes of Taber around these parts. They get their pleasures out of hangin' innocent folks. Sam Averill ought to know better."

"I don't think Sam Averill realizes what his detective is up to," Schmidt said. "Anyway, remember what I said about the widow."

"That's between you and me," Buchanan replied.

Bert Schmidt left the emporium and drove the Belgian back to the mill. He couldn't ride down to Sam Averill's Triple S ranch right away because of the storm, but as soon as the weather cleared . . .

VIII

CYRUS Taber did not like to lose. When he caught O. B. Webster red-handed, he knew he had caught himself a two-bit rustler. Ordinarily, such an event wouldn't have stirred Taber's blood much. The two hundred dollars was a fine padding against the coming winter, but to be able to nail the hide of someone like Bert Schmidt to the door—that was something to contemplate with pleasure. The trouble was, Taber now knew that unless Schmidt was the world's finest actor, he was innocent as snow.

But someone had put the finish to Webster's miserable life and the range detective found himself fascinated by the possibilities. As far as he knew, Webster hadn't had a chance to blab to anyone once they had ridden into town. Maybe he'd found time to slip out the back of the cabin while Taber waited under the trees. That was possible, but one thing was sure—no one had seen them ride into Williams that night.

The more he thought about it, the more puzzled the detective became. There were other rustlers out there to be found before winter set in for good. Taber knew he should be seeking better hunting to the south, but something told him to keep after this affair. And who knows, he thought . . . there might come a time to pay back that damned fast-fisted logger.

Taber put his weight on the stirrups and eased up out of the saddle. He still ached enough to keep the memory of that thrashing alive. He'd spent the previous night at the small boarding house in Williams owned by the galoot who ran the emporium next door. The bed was uncomfortable, the room freezing. Wind leaked in through a hundred places. It had been like sleeping in a snow drift, which Taber had done more than once. He rode out of Williams, intending to reach Averill's ranch by nightfall.

Several miles south of Williams Peak, the mountains began to give way to a series of low, rolling hills that merged into the gentle swell of the prairie. Taber cursed the wind that still gusted from the northwest. Behind each snowy bush lay a long-tailed drift. Rises in the land had been blown nearly clear. The snow filled the dips and blemishes, giving the prairie a burnished appearance. The brightness hurt his eyes. Once clear of the mountains, the detective steered a course that would cross the narrow-gauge railroad. His horse crested a low rise after a couple of hours, and before them were the tracks. The ties were snow-covered, but here and there the rust brown of the rails shown through the white of the snow.

For a man to build maybe thirty miles of private railroad, Taber thought, there must be a hell of a lot of money in trees and lumber. When the trees were gone, the thirty miles of rails would be ripped up, leaving a trail of rotting ties across the prairie. Taber had seen it done before.

He rode directly to the tracks and let his horse follow the rails, walking along the side of the narrow roadbed. He could follow those tracks for several miles before he had to veer again to the west toward Averill's spread. Even with the snow drifted on the leeward of the rails, walking was easier, and Taber's horse made comfortable progress. For his part, Taber looped the reins around the saddle horn and let the animal find its own way. He sat with arms tightly folded across his chest, gloved hands buried under his arms for warmth.

After a time, a sound other than the wind through the sage and the snow pellets skittering along the iron rails attracted Taber's attention. He unfolded his arms and picked up the reins, then checked them lightly, bringing the palomino to a halt. He turned in the saddle. Behind him, still several miles distant, he could see a black smudge rising and then pulled apart by the wind, and the wind carried the metallic clankings and rattlings of the locomotive to his ears. The engineer was not sparing the pine knots. After a while, Taber could see the engine and its train of four small flatcars and one boxcar clearly. From the inverted bell stack, flame and sparks shot up with the smoke, and as the train approached, Taber saw the engine and cars lurching from side to side as imperfections in the roadbed threw the machine's weight. The detective urged his horse down off the roadbed and away from the tracks. Already, the animal was nervous. Taber gripped the reins tightly as the train approached, expecting the worst from the excited palomino. He was not disappointed. When two hundred yards distant, the engine's whistle let out a series of piercing blasts, and Taber's horse kicked snow in every direction. Taber sat out the palomino's gyrations, trying only to prevent the horse from bolting.

When the locomotive shot past at twenty-five miles an hour, the skittish palomino had moved a hundred yards from the tracks. The engineer waved a hand in greeting and Taber replied in kind. The four flatcars, much smaller than those he had seen on the bigger lines, were loaded high with timber and lumber, all lashed down with chains.

It was not the engine or the lumber on the flatcars that caught Taber's attention as the train clattered past, nor the sparks and billowing black smoke from the stack. As the train flew by, Taber heard the unmistakable bawl of cattle. He sat up straight in the saddle. With narrowed eyes he watched the receding boxcar.

"Why, that son of a bitch," he said aloud. Without thinking, he spurred his anxious horse into a wild, snow-kicking gallop across the prairie and up onto the side of the now freshly marked roadbed. He raced after the train, but it was a useless pursuit. The train steadily drew away, taking advantage of the slight downgrade of the prairie that ran away from the mountains. After a minute of dangerous riding, Taber pulled his horse back to a dancing trot, and then to a walk. Finally, he pulled the palomino to a halt and sat quietly, watching the train shrink in the distance.

"It's more than lumber you're shipping, Mister Bert Schmidt," Taber muttered. The railhead was more than fifteen miles away, but the range detective once more kicked his horse into motion, urging the animal into a ground-eating canter. When he reached the spot where he would have to leave the railbed and strike out west for Averill's, he ignored that path and stuck to the tracks. By keeping up the pace and not sparing his horse, he might arrive at the railhead soon enough after the train to discover something very interesting. As the wind of his passage stung his cheeks, Taber grinned to himself. The train would reach the station at least an hour before him, but even so, the hunt was far from finished.

The railhead at Littel nestled at the foot of Thunder Butte, a flat , tabletop of rock-strewn land that lofted six hundred feet above the prairie. Thunder Butte offered little other than protection from the prevailing winds. Littel served a handful of ranchers, a few miners and other entre-preneurs, and Bert Schmidt.

"Railhead" was an exaggeration, since Littel was no more than a single siding off the main east-west line. A single, large, and well-built corral served as a holding pen for livestock. At times, as many as a thousand head waited their turn at the cattlecars. Schmidt's narrow-gauge track wound around the butte, passed before the corral, paralleled the siding track, and then ended a hundred feet past the corral. There was no way to turn the small locomotive around. Schmidt had decided against the extra track and switches to do that when he'd discovered that the small engine ran as well backwards as forwards. As a result, Schmidt's engine chugged into Littel pulling its five cars and left the next morning, running backwards, pushing the cars back up to Williams Peak.

That day, when Phillip Scott fed the knots to the locomotive and rounded the butte, his first sight was of the Union Pacific engine and its line of cars waiting at the siding. He sighed with relief. It took a big storm to halt those locomotives. To them, the recent snowfall was of no consequence. He reached up, pulled the cord, and the engine let out a screech.

Perhaps a hundred head of cattle were in the pens as Scott slowed the engine. He watched them being fed up the cattle chute and into waiting cars, each animal trudging across the narrow-gauge tracks. Further down, nearly at the end of the siding, two flatcars waited. As always, Scott looked with some envy at the Union Pacific rig. He'd heard of some of the larger engines up north pulling a mile-long train of cattle cars. The engine parked that day, steam gently wisping from its cylinders, no doubt weighed as much as ten engines such as Scott was used to. Some of them, he knew, could reach as much as sixty miles an hour, maybe more. He tooted the whistle once more and the cowpunchers stopped loading to let him pass. With help from his fireman, Luke Tate, the engineer guided the small locomotive past the yards.

Finally, the narrow-gauge came to a steaming halt. Scott halted his train when the lumber cars were directly opposite the mainline flatcars. And it was no accident that the double side doors of the boxcar stopped opposite one of the entry chutes to the main railhead corral. That car was emptied by two men before the tie-downs around the lumber were loosened. Sixteen head of cattle joined the milling herd in the corrals. With all the rest, they were goaded into the large cars of the mainline train. It had taken just eight minutes to off load the steers. And during that time Phillip Scott and Luke Tate never gave the small boxcar more than a passing glance. Instead, they busied themselves with the lumber transfer, assisted by half a dozen men from the Union Pacific train.

In another twenty minutes, all the cattle were confined in the darkness of the cars and the doors were slammed shut. To the north of the cattle yard stood a simple sod hut—the station house. It was there that anyone staying the night would rest. Scott didn't relish the thought. Had the rear car of his train born a spotlight, he would have made the return trip that night. Scott glanced up and saw a heavy-set man coming from the hut. The engineer stopped work and clambered down from the flatcar to meet him.

The man greeted Scott and nodded at the boxcar. "Brought that along, eh? Right smart, this kind of weather. Folks are going to be eager for that coal. You want to load this afternoon, or are you going to wait for mornin'?"

"Tomorrow," Scott said. "We'll be another couple hours at it now, then we'll back the engine out of your way." He nodded at the station. Beside the building and covered with snow was a fair-sized pile of burlap sacks. Each one contained a hundredweight of coal.

"Damned wasteful way to ship coal, if you ask me," the man said.

"Customer wants it that way," Scott replied with a shrug. "Easier for him to sell that way, and he can afford to save himself some work." He glanced at the man. "He pays for it, and still makes a buck or two. I don't guess he needs to worry none about money."

"No, he don't," the man nodded. "Well, you just back up when you're ready. Don't forget to come inside and sign for it. You be stayin' the night, then?"

"We will. I ain't about to run blind back up the mountain."

The man shook his head. "Don't see how you can see much of anything, daylight or no, goin' backwards like that."

Scott grinned. "This train ain't so big a man can't see by it."

"Suppose not." He paused and looked over at the other

men who were working with the lumber shipment. He lowered his voice. "Sixteen, was it?"

Scott nodded, and then clapped his gloved hands together. "Well," he said, "talkin' ain't gonna get that lumber off." He turned and went back to work.

Luck was not with Cyrus Taber. He'd made rapid progress and was following the tracks toward the north end of Thunder Butte, only three miles from Littel, when his horse planted a hoof awkwardly and plunged off-balance. Before the palomino could regain its balance, it had clattered across the steel rails, finishing up on its knees with its muzzle all but dug into the snow. Taber relaxed the reins and let the animal rear back up on its feet. When the palomino took the first tentative steps after the fall, it limped heavily. Taber cursed and swung down from the saddle. He examined the animal's front legs and found an ugly scrape on the left pastern. He cursed again and remounted. After that, he was forced to ride into Littel at little more than a walk.

Half of the coal sacks had been tossed into the boxcar when Phillip Scott looked up and saw the lone figure riding slowly toward the depot. The palomino was limping.

"Now who might that be?" Tate asked, seeing the rider.

Scott squinted and recognition crossed his face. "He was by the tracks when we passed up on Averill range a ways back. Must be one of his men."

"What's he doing down here?"

Scott shrugged and grabbed another sack. Cyrus Taber rode slowly up to the train and stopped near the back of the boxcar, surveying the working men calmly.

"Howdy," he said.

Scott waved a hand and continued work. "You've come a piece," he said. "Horse comin' up lame?"

Taber swung down from the saddle. "Slipped back a few miles. Fell on the tracks. Just a bruise, I think."

"Bad weather to have a horse come up lame," Scott said.

Taber walked his horse forward and stood just to one side of the open boxcar door. He peered inside at the sacks. "What's all this?"

"Coal," Tate said. "Mike Buchanan up in Williams ordered hisself coal—all bagged up and fancy like." He heaved a heavy sack inside the car. "Never seen the like."

Taber nodded. "What do you do, run this car down empty just to pick up this load?"

"Yep."

"That's quite a load of timber you boys brought down, too. That Bert Schmidt's doing?"

"Yep. He ships every few weeks, weather allowin'. Sometimes more."

Taber leaned so he could see inside the boxcar, but he stayed out of the men's way. To himself, he cursed his luck at arriving late. He eyed the sacks, piled nearly to the roof, filling the car from one end to the other. Black dust had sifted through the coarse burlap. It mixed with the snow and turned it gray. He looked down and something caught his eye. He reached into the car with one hand and scraped some of the cattle dung off the floor near the doorsill. It was fresh. He held up his gloved hand and turned and looked at the man nearest him. Phillip Scott's face remained blank.

"Just bringing down lumber, you say." Taber held his gloved hand with the manure on the finger tips and Scott's eyes went first from that evidence to Taber's face.

"That's right," the engineer said.

"Where are the cattle?" Taber asked. His voice was quiet.

"There's about a hundred head of them over in that there train, if you're of a mind to collect their leavings," Scott said. "Or you can scrape off the boots of any man working on the loading." He swung another sack up into the car for emphasis, and it landed with a thud.

"I'll want to see them."

"Then you just go ahead," Scott replied and promptly

ignored the man. Taber turned on his heel, picked up the palomino's reins, and walked the length of the train, crossing in front of the engine. He walked along the Union Pacific cars, looking closely. Four of them were loaded with shifting, bellowing cattle. A man wearing a black derby approached from the direction of the hissing engine. Taber saw the man's liberal coating of coal dust and guessed he was either the fireman or the engineer.

"I need to see these cattle," Taber said.

"That right? And just who might you be?"

"Name's Cyrus Taber. Range detective. I work for Sam Averill, up north."

"That right." The man spat tobacco juice into the snow. "Just which cow did you want to see?"

Taber held the reins of his horse in his left hand, and his right stayed near the split pocket of his greatcoat. "I want to see the steers that came off the narrow-gauge."

The engineer looked genuinely puzzled. He had not seen the steers unloaded, and had no reason to believe there had been any. "Only thing came off that train was lumber, pal," he said.

"I want to see the steers."

The engineer pulled out his pocket watch. "Well, I tell you what. I got about seven minutes before we're pulling on out of this little shit-hole. If you can unload them cars, and have 'em loaded again in seven minutes, you're welcome to look all you like. Otherwise, you're just plumb out of luck. 'Course," and he smiled helpfully, "you can ride on into Thatcher. We'll be stoppin' there for a few minutes to take on water. And then on into Laramie. Stockyard's there. That's where these critters are gettin' off." He spat again. "For a time, anyways."

"I'll put my horse aboard and go with you."

The engineer shook his head. "Ain't got no room for that horse. You either. Less you want to freeze your ass off ridin' atop that lumber. Can't have that, though."

"Then I want to look in those cars."

"Mister, you're a bit on the thick-headed side. Them four cars are about to bust at the seams. I ain't about to open them doors, because if I do, them cows'll come out." He spoke as if he was addressing a child. "Now, you got two choices. You can open the roof vent and shinny down inside, and walk across them cows' backs 'til you find what you're after, or you can ride to Laramie and watch 'em unload there. That's if that lame horse of yours can run forty mile an hour for a hundred-and-fifty mile or more. I seen that animal limpin' when you walked up this way. I'd say, if I was you, that you'd best attend to your problems. Unless you live in these parts, you got some walkin' to do. I wouldn't worry so much about cows." He spat and regarded Taber's darkening face with infuriating calmness.

Taber considered, briefly, forcing the unloading of the train. The engineer wasn't wearing a gun, but some of the others down the track were. Taber was alone and it would be impossible to watch his backside during the operation. He let the idea drop.

"I'll see your shipping manifest, then," Taber said. A muscle in his jaw twitched.

"Show me your badge, friend," the engineer said. "If you're a United States marshal, you can see anything you like. Might even hold up the schedule for you, for maybe thirty, forty seconds. Otherwise, you're shit out of luck." The engineer spat again. Before Taber could reply, the big engine let out a loud whoop from its whistle. "Steam's up," the engineer said. "Unless you got other business, I wish you the best of luck, friend." He grinned cheerfully and left Taber in a fury.

In minutes, the mammoth drive wheels of the mainliner spun against the polished tracks, then caught hold. Slowly, groaning and creaking with the bellow of cattle mixed in, the train eased down the siding and onto the main track. It paused long enough for a man to leap down from the caboose. He ran down the track a short distance and threw the massive handle of the siding switch, then sprinted back to the caboose. The train accelerated and in a while was nothing but a speck, rocking from side to side down the tracks and into the distance. All the while, Taber stood helplessly, jaw knotted and eyes squinting.

As if to add insult, the small whistle of the narrow-gauge hooted, and Taber turned to see it backing up its tracks.

Inside the small engine, Tate was frowning. "It's going to be goddamned cold hangin' onto that boxcar with one hand and a lantern in the other, come dark," he muttered.

"We ain't got much choice, now," Scott replied. "But we got a while before it gets dark." He was craning his neck and watching the tracks as the train backed around the end of Thunder Butte.

"Schmidt'll have our ass," Tate said

Scott shot a glance at his partner. "It ain't Bert Schmidt I'm worryin' about. Worst will happen is some steer'll wander on the tracks and get clipped. That's a chance I'll take."

"Maybe we can just tell him the weather looked like it was brewin' somethin'!"

"Like I said," Scott replied, shouting to be heard over the laboring engine, "I ain't worried about what Bert Schmidt'll say. You just keep that boiler fed."

IX

THERE was no moon. Clouds hung so low over the peaks that at times, as he stumbled through the snow under the trees without aid of a lantern's light, Phillip Scott thought there was no sky at all. The wind had let up, though, and the mountains were deathly still.

It wasn't long, especially after a hard day and a hastily bolted supper, before Scott was chilled to the bone. The dark building loomed before him. He found the thick door and knocked, stamping his feet impatiently. Finally, the door opened a crack. A narrow shaft of light illuminated Scott's face, but the door opened no further.

"I said I didn't want to see you," a voice said.

"I got to talk to you," Scott replied quickly. He pushed at the door. It opened enough for the man inside to slip out. He closed the door, putting himself and Scott in darkness.

"Then we'll talk out here," he said. "Now what do you want? Make it snappy."

"You know that range detectice Averill hired?"

"Yes."

"When we took the engine down today, he was out on the prairie, by the tracks."

"So?"

"I mean, I think he heard the cattle. He must have knowed, 'cause he rode down to the railhead. Got there just as we was finishin' loadin' the coal."

"Did he see anything?"

"He saw the manure in the boxcar. Asked where the cattle was."

"What did you say?"

"I said there weren't no cattle. Said the manure came from some of the men's boots. But then he went and talked with the Union Pacific people. Don't know what he asked 'em, but they didn't give him the time of day. He didn't get inside any of their cars."

"The railroad people know nothing about it. Neither does Taber."

"I ain't so sure, now. This Taber's no fool. Me and Tate, we pulled out, instead of stayin' the night, like usual."

"That was stupid, Scott. He had nothing on you. You should have acted like usual. Like nothin' was wrong."

"Didn't seem so at the time."

"Seems to me runnin' a train at night, ass backwards, with no lights, is enough to tell the whole world somethin's wrong. Next time, use your damned head."

"I ain't sure there'll be a next time. Not with the weather settin' in like it is."

"One more load. I'll let you know when. And Scott . . . " The man reached out and laid a hand on Scott's shoulder like they were brothers. "Leave Mister Taber to me."

"You sure about that?"

"I'm sure. I got a feelin' he won't bother us much more."

X

FOR two days, only one thing had been on Bert Schmidt's mind. Since he hadn't seen Cyrus Taber in days, and because of nagging problems at the mill, his temper had cooled to the point where he had almost forgotten the detective. What bothered him now was the presence of Carlotta Webster a half a mile down the hill.

Schmidt was still old-fashioned enough to believe that solitary women were helpless. That Sunday morning he sat in his cabin with the coffee pot warming on the top of the big potbellied stove. Schmidt made an entry for November 21, 1886, in his diary, writing in small, fine script with black ink and a scratchy steel pen. One entry revealed his concern: "I wonder how the Webster woman can face the winter."

Schmidt pictured Carlotta's face, her tousled hair. How could a woman like her get hitched with a man like O. B. Webster? Webster might have been a handsome enough man at one time, but as a provider he was useless.

Thank God the woman didn't have half a dozen children hanging from her apron.

"A fine looking woman," he wrote. "She has a good head on her shoulders, and should make do all right."

He paused, skipped a line, and made another entry or two, then snapped the diary closed. He put it back on the shelf in line with his father's and grandfather's. He then pulled down a battered Bible and returned to his chair. Bert Schmidt couldn't abide attending church. He didn't mind the mild sermons delivered by the quiet pastor, Harold Gilmore, but Schmidt's relationship was with God alone. It was between the two of them.

He read for perhaps ten minutes, but Carlotta Webster kept intruding. He closed the Bible and put it back on the shelf. He walked to the window and looked at the thermometer. The sky was still leaden, the snow had no sparkle.

"Wonder if she's got enough wood," he muttered to himself. That notion gave him something to do. He put on his coat, hat, gloves, and boots and left his cabin. He walked quickly to the stable behind the sawmill and harnessed the Belgian to the freight wagon, then drove the rig to the towering pile of chips and slab wood behind the mill. Working steadily, he began to fill the wagon, avoiding pieces that were heavy with bark or too long. After an hour, he straightened up and surveyed his handiwork. The sides of the wagon were just eighteen inches high. The wood arched from side to side, a full three feet high in the middle. "That ought to do it," he said. He slapped his gloves together and swung up on the seat. With a gentle tap of the reins, the big Belgian stepped out. The path down to the village was well-packed. The Belgian kept its head down, and eyed the slippery ground, its shoes of cleated iron gripping the ice. Before long, they were in front of the Webster cabin. Schmidt looped the reins over the brake handle and hopped down. After knocking on the door, he waited for several minutes. Finally the door opened and Carlotta peered out uncertainly. She saw Schmidt and smiled, showing fine, even teeth.

"Why, Mister Schmidt," she said nervously.

"I brought down this load of chips from the mill. Figured maybe you could use some, weather being what it is."

She looked past him to the loaded wagon. "That's very kind of you." Then her eyes lit up. "What a fine horse."

Schmidt turned and looked at the Belgian. "Yep. Getting on in years, though. Used to be one of my timber haulers, but we turned him out to pasture." He grinned at Carlotta. "This here is play to him, not work. Where would be a good spot to put those chips?"

The woman hesitated. "It's most kind of you, Mister Schmidt, but I have no money . . ." She stopped, embarrassed.

"Oh, the wood's not for sale. No, ma'am. You'd do me a kindness to take it off my hands. See, up at the mill, there's a pile a thousand times that little load. And it just keeps growing on us. So you'd be doing me a favor."

"You're sure?"

"Oh, yes. There's a number of folks in town who come up and get their own. 'Course, you don't have a wagon, and I was coming this way, so I just thought maybe you'd be able to use some, too."

"That's very kind of you," she said again. She was wearing a long gingham dress and there was admiration in Schmidt's eyes when he looked at her.

"Well then, you just tell me where you want it."

"Would it be possible to put it behind the cabin? Near the kitchen door?"

"I should think so. Let me walk around and see what we got." Schmidt touched the fur of his cap and then trudged through the small drifts to the back of the cabin. Beside the door was a full rain barrel. The water was frozen for the first few inches and was pushing at the staves. Carlotta opened the back door just as Schmidt was eyeing the barrel critically.

"How about right here?" he said, gesturing. "Be easy to get at."

"That would be fine."

"Turns warmer, you might want to empty that," Schmidt said, pointing at the barrel. "Won't be worth much if you don't. That ice'll burst the barrel." Carlotta started to say something but she just nodded instead. "I'll fetch the wagon."

Two large blackjacks prevented him from just driving around the cabin, so he pulled the wagon abreast of the trees and then tugged gently on the reins. The singletree of the wagon groaned as the big horse pressed backwards. The Belgian backed the heavy wagon into the narrow spot, halting just as the tailgate touched the trees. By that time, Carlotta had her coat on. She and Schmidt made rapid work of unloading.

"There, now," Schmidt said.

"That's wonderful," Carlotta said. Her flushed cheeks made her eyes seem all the more blue.

"Well, like I say, you don't have to ration it. I got a mountain of it needs a home still."

"I don't know how to thank you."

"No need," Schmidt said with a wave of his hand. "Load of wood chips isn't much." He moved toward the front of the wagon. "You need anything, just holler." Carlotta watched him swing up into the seat and gather the reins. She knew she should invite him inside, maybe offer him coffee, but she couldn't bring herself to make the invitation. Not yet. Bert Schmidt was such a pleasant, self-assured man, she thought. But not yet. So, instead she merely smiled her thanks to him and Schmidt nodded and chucked the reins.

After he was gone, she gathered up an awkward armload of the chips and went inside. In moments, her home was nearly bursting with warmth. It was the first decent fire she'd had in four days, built with something other than the squaw wood she'd managed to break from the lower limbs of trees. Her husband had always hated to cut firewood and invariably waited until the first storm of winter before laying down a cord.

While working with Schmidt, Carlotta's sadness had diminished some. But now, memories of her husband flooded back and she sat with her head in her hands.

"Give it time," the parson's wife, Milly Gilmore, had said. She was rumored to be a wise woman, and maybe she was right, after all. If this hot, sparking fire was the first sign, maybe she was right.

XI

SHORTLY before noon on November 26, Bert Schmidt
finished a frustrating session with his timber foreman, Stan
Chester. A bridge needed building, a job that should have
been completed early in the fall. The bridge was to span a
gully between two ridges that teams couldn't cross. But Stan
Chester was no engineer. He could coax work from his crews
in any weather, could thread a team of eight oxen through
dense timber without pause, could drop a giant fir on target,
but when it came to measuring and fitting pieces of wood he
was hopeless. The position of the diagonal bracing under
the main spars of the bridge was ruled by common sense,
Schmidt had thought. Apparently not, for Chester had
placed the supports where they would do the least good—
adding weight but no strength. After five hours, he finally
felt it safe to leave Chester on his own.

"I have it now," Chester said more than once, nodding
vigorously. Sure enough, he did, finally. By the end of the
day, the oxen would be trudging across the freshly split
surfaces of the cross-logs.

Schmidt rode back to the mill through areas already
harvested. An army of stumps jutted out of the snow.
Schmidt was reminded that his years on Williams Peak were
limited. When the time came, he would strip the mill, loading the equipment behind his locomotive. Then, he and his
crew would head for the main line, and as the engine and its
cars passed for the last time down the narrow-gauge, the
rails would be torn up, leaving the cross-ties to slowly decay.
Everything would go with him, including the locomotive, all
loaded on the big Union Pacific trains, heading west to the

coast, and then north to the big timber country. But all that was five, maybe six years down the road. Williams Peak still had timber to offer, and Schmidt meant to take all of it.

The fantasies of redwoods and sequoias were on Schmidt's mind as he reached the sawmill. As he reined in beside the stable he saw a graceful palomino standing patiently by the end wall of the mill. He put his own Belgian in the stall and walked quickly to the mill. As he entered the lunch whistle shrieked and the din of the saws wound down. Gingras met him as he walked around the saw carriage.

"Did you get Chester straightened out?" Gingras asked with a grin.

"Hope so. Whose horse is that outside?"

"Ah," Gingras said. "You have a visitor. He is in the office." A half smile spread on the Frenchman's big face. "I don't know how happy you will be to see him."

"Oh?" Schmidt said. He walked rapidly past the silent saws and reached the open door of his office. Standing inside, scanning Schmidt's papers, was Cyrus Taber. Schmidt halted, hands on his hips. "What the hell are you after now?"

Taber turned. "We need to talk."

Schmidt slammed the door behind him and glared. "Maybe you can start by telling me why you told the widow Webster I killed her husband."

Taber appraised Schmidt cooly. His sheepskin coat was unbuttoned, his right hand near the butt of a revolver. "I never told her that."

Schmidt stepped closer. "Then how'd she come by the idea? She came up here to settle accounts with me."

Taber shrugged. "Distressed women, they don't think straight." Schmidt glared at Taber silently, then grunted in disgust as he crossed the small room and sat down.

Satisfied that Schmidt's mood wouldn't blossom into vio- lence, Taber said, "Quite an operation you have here." When Schmidt didn't reply, he added, "I decided to come and make peace." Schmidt glanced up warily, for men like Taber usually didn't apologize for anything they did, especially after a beating. "I figure I was wrong about you," Taber continued. "And in a country like this, a man doesn't need any more enemies than he collects naturally."

"That all you came to say?" Schmidt's voice was flat and emotionless.

One of Taber's eyebrows lifted fractionally. "Yes. I guess it is."

"Then you can leave." Schmidt stood and rested a hand on the table in front of him. "And tell Sam Averill I still intend to see him about what happened."

"He would have come up," Taber lied, "but you know how it is, weather and all." The truth was that Cyrus Taber had never mentioned the incident to Averill at all. Taber had not been back to the Triple S since the day he'd caught Webster with the rustled beef. The range detective moved back to the door of the office and hesitated. "That's quite a locomotive you have, Mister Schmidt."

"Yes, it is."

"You run down to the railhead often?"

"When there's need."

Taber watched Schmidt's face closely and said, "I was out on the prairie, south of here, last week. Saw the train heading down." Schmidt's face remained impassive. Taber smiled. "Rate it was running on those tracks, I found myself wishing I was aboard, rather than on my horse."

It was no liking of Taber that prompted Schmidt to say what he did, just the thought of anyone out on the wind-swept prairie in winter. "Anyone wants to ride down to the railhead on the engine is welcome," he said. "When there's room."

Taber's pulse quickened. "I don't think I could get my horse to stand still on one of those flatcars," he said.

"There's the boxcar. It goes down when there's a load coming back from the railhead that wants to be protected from the elements."

"I may take you up on that."

Schmidt looked sharply at Taber. "It wasn't an offer, Taber. What you do is no concern of mine. You want to ride that train, do it. Just don't come to me about it. The less I see of you, the better I like it." He nodded at the waiting door.

"As you like," Taber said slowly. He left the mill and mounted his horse. Beyond the stables, he could see the locomotive sitting under the protection of the open-ended shed. The roof spanned just enough to cover the engine and tender. The remaining cars stretched out behind, empty. As Taber rode past, he looked at the boxcar carefully. If that train so much as budged an inch, Taber thought, he would know it. No matter how long it took, he would know. He was a patient man.

He rode down into Williams, feeling pleased with himself. He went to the emporium and sat at one of the tables away from the bar. The place was all but empty, and after one of the girls who worked there brought Taber a hot bowl of stew, Mike Buchanan wandered over.

"You want something to drink?" the big bartender asked.

"No . . . obliged," Taber replied and began to eat. He looked up at Buchanan, swallowed, and said, "It's on the warm side in here." Indeed, it was. The stove glowed cherry red and a pot of water on top of it burbled happily.

Buchanan swelled with pride. "Yep. Warmest spot in the Rocky Mountains. That's coal, you see," he smiled widely. "Just shovel 'er in and let 'er rip."

"You selling a lot of it?"

"Oh, some," Buchanan said easily. "Takes folks a time to get used to the notion. Isn't anything new about coal, you understand. Just that most folks persist with the idea that wood does just as good. It don't, and after a time, why, they find that out and come back for more." He grinned. "It's a convenience, you know. Folks around here aren't used to the modern way of life. Hard as this winter's going to be, they'll learn." Taber nodded and watched Buchanan as the big man walked to the stove and opened the door. He bent down, rattled the grate, peered inside again, and closed the door. "Burns damned near forever," he said, wiping his hands. "I'm thinking that maybe I ought to order me another load, just so's folks aren't cut short."

"You have it brought up on the narrow-gauge?"

"Oh, hell yes. Can't carry enough on a wagon to spit at." He looked at the stove judiciously, then glanced at Taber. "Yup. I think that when old Schmidt makes his run, I'll do just that."

Taber was interested, but not in coal. "How often does he go down?"

Buchanan shrugged. "He don't have a set schedule. Whenever he feels the need, or has himself an order to ship. One of his boys workin' the engine was sayin' he thought they'd have a load in a week, maybe two. Maybe sooner. This time of year, he begins to do more millin' than timber work. Snow gets so deep the teams can't haul out them big logs. By February, he'll be runnin' down nearly once a week." Buchanan grinned and shook his head. "I always wanted to ride that thing. Never had the time. Course, there ain't much down there unless you want to catch the Union Pacific."

Taber nodded absently and pushed his plate away. He was still puzzled about Bert Schmidt. Rustlers didn't behave like he did. But one thing pleased Taber: it couldn't be a one man operation. There would be many times the amount he'd received for catching O. B. Webster. Folks in Williams would have to figure some other way to get their coal. Cyrus Taber was going to put that train out of business.

XII

TABER'S hands shook slightly from nervous anticipation. It was not yet dawn, and the weather was nasty. Taber knelt under the ice-laden boughs of a double-trunked pine and ignored the wind and the sting of snow. In the days previous, he had scouted carefully, following the tracks of the narrow-gauge. To his knowledge, he had neither been seen nor heard. But careful as he was, he had almost missed it. Seven miles south of the mill, where the flank of Williams Peak swept down into a series of draws, the tracks headed toward the southern prairie.

One narrow draw was nearly blocked by boulders where the railroad cut passed through. It was in this gully that the range detective found the freshly cut pine poles. The poles lay helter-skelter, mixed with the rest of the deadfall and brush. But no snow covered them—no old snow. Taber had circled his horse through the area. The palomino's prints had mixed with those of cattle, deer, elk, and coyotes. Taber grinned. He had found a corral site that had been used recently and would be used again. The poles could be thrown up in a moment's notice. He could see no post holes, but he knew they would be there if he looked hard enough. It took Taber only five minutes to walk his horse from the would-be corral to the narrow-gauge.

The range detective stood beside his horse in the snow and looked back at his tracks. The lay of the land was perfect. Taber reasoned that whoever was rustling the cattle herded the animals to that remote spot—a spot protected in every direction from casual discovery. When the narrow-gauge train chugged down the mountain, it would take just mo-

77

ments to herd the cattle down the draw and into the boxcar. From there, it was a nearly straight shot to the railhead. It was a two-bit operation, Taber had mused. No more than a dozen cattle—maybe eighteen at the most—could be carried in the boxcar at one time. No more than two cowboys would be needed.

Taber knew the train would make a run on the sixth of December. After discovering the corral site, he began to keep watch on the locomotive. He found a spot up the hill and to the west where he could see the activity at the mill from behind a stand of gooseberry bushes and slender blackjacks. He listened to the distant sounds of the mill hands as they yelled back and forth.

On December 4, Taber rode south to the Averill ranch. He knew his own capabilities well, and trusted himself, but had no desire to face half a dozen men alone.

He described what he had learned. Rustlers weren't on the rancher's mind, the weather was. It was cold, and had been for days. There was no promise of anything better. Snow spat almost daily and the wind constantly whipped the snow into small blizzards that made any ranch work a chore. Water holes froze. Sutton Creek itself was crusting at the edges and icing across where the water was quiet and pooled. Sam Averill was thinking about January and February when Taber visited his ranch. Nevertheless, when Taber rode back toward Williams, he had two of Averill's best men with him. Thomas Burke, the Triple S foreman, was eager and willing, and Averill grudgingly let him go. Taber had worked with Burke before and knew him to be quick and competent with a gun. Burke was an even-tempered thirty-one years old. In addition, Averill sent Borden Payne, a forty-one year old veteran of trail drives, blizzards, and Indian wars.

Late in the afternoon of December 5, the three men reached the rolling foothills south of Williams Peak. Light snow was again sifting across the prairies. The night promised to be cold. Because they wanted to be sure they wouldn't miss, Taber and his companions settled into crevices and nooks in the rocks near the tracks. They had buffalo robes with them, and they waited. In the dim light of the morning, the robes covered with snow, they were all but invisible.

Sometime early that morning, the three men heard the sounds that told them they had come to the right place. Up the draw came the deep, hollow sound of wood on wood. Taber shifted under his robe and smiled. He carefully unwrapped and moved to the shelter of the double-trunked pine further up the hill. The light was still so dim that footing was treacherous.

The horses were quiet. Taber, Burke, and Payne had left their mounts in a dense grove of young timber beyond the brow of the hill.

When it was light enough for a man to be able to walk across the rough and slippery terrain without falling on his face, the first bellowing of cattle on the move swelled through the air.

At almost the same instant, the heavy breathing of the steam locomotive was carried down from the peak. Taber guessed that it was nearly six o'clock. There was not much time. As the locomotive drew nearer, Taber shivered. He was tense and eager.

To the north, above the crowns of the trees, smoke spurted up, marking the passage of the engine. Simultaneously, Taber heard voices. He craned his neck and watched the draw. A dozen or so cattle were being herded toward the tracks by two men.

Despite himself, Taber marveled at the men's planning. They did not push the cattle directly to the tracks, away from the draw's cover, until the engine had hissed itself to a stop. Taber could see the engineer in the cab of the locomotive. He held his breath. Burke and Payne held their fire. Before any move was made, Taber wanted the cattle loaded in the car. It would make his job so much easier. Besides, men always stopped to talk. There would be time.

As the train pulled to a stop, the double doors of the boxcar slid open on well-greased tracks. Instantly, the small ramp for the cattle was shoved out and one end thudded into the snow. The two drovers rode quickly, pressing the cattle toward the car. Several of the steers balked but the horsemen were always ready. It took no more than a few minutes for the cattle to clamber into the car. The sides of the ramp kept them in line. Once the steers were inside, the man who had been in the boxcar heaved the ramp back into the car, slammed the doors closed, and sprinted to one of the flat-cars. He hurried for good reason. Even as the hooves of the last steer were scrabbling on the ramp, the engineer was feeding steam to the engine. The two rustling cowpunchers wheeled their mounts and raced up the draw.

Taber was not quick enough. He had not expected such a smooth operation and in the few seconds it took him and his two companions to stumble down from the rocks, their quarries were nearly out of range.

"We didn't move until we saw you," Burke shouted, and Taber cursed. Taber had been skunked.

"Get to the horses," he yelled and ran up the hill. He slipped and slid and more than once barked his shins on hidden stumps or rocks. As they crested the rise and started down to the copse of blackjacks where their horses were hidden, Taber shouted instructions. "Burke, you head after that train. You can catch it before it gets down on the open prairie. If not, go on down to the railhead. Payne and I will track those other two." And then, as they came to the horses, the three men abruptly stopped.

Standing beside their horses was a lone man with a rifle. He moved so fast that Taber had no chance to realize that his own plans had been no secret at all. The stranger's weapon bellowed and Taber was flung sideways into the snow, his own rifle buried underneath him. Neither Burke nor Borden Payne was a professional fighter and their stunned hesitation was fatal. Burke fumbled under his coat for his six-gun, but a bullet smashed him backwards.

"Jesus!" It was Borden Payne. He swung his ponderous buffalo gun up. The rifle crashed again and Payne went to his knees with a gasp. Both hands clasped the front of his coat. The buffalo gun sank out of sight.

The shots came so fast that the wounded Taber heard them only as one continuous sound. His right side was numb. He heard the soft crunch of boots in snow and he struggled to push himself up. By turning his head he could see Payne. The older man was still on his knees, rocking slightly in agony with his hands clutching the hide of his heavy coat. The man with the rifle walked slowly to Payne and the eyes of the two men met. The rifle rose slowly until its muzzle was just above Payne's gloved hands, just inches from the center of his chest. The explosion was deafening and Payne was blown backwards, his arms flung out in the snow. Cyrus Taber struggled to move, to regain his own rifle, but his right arm was useless.

With a tremendous effort, he managed to roll over on his back, breathing heavily.

"You son of a bitch," he groaned. He looked up at the pale gray morning light. There was nothing he could do, and Cyrus Taber knew it. He realized that, without any doubt, this was his last morning on earth.

"Don't shoot me any more," he murmured. "You got what you wanted."

The man shook his head slowly. "You hang on too tight, Taber." He held the rifle in one hand, almost negligently. Taber sat up with a lurch. The blast of the rifle knocked him back down. He screamed, but the cry was cut off abruptly by another hammering blow, and then another. Taber felt as if his body were suspended several inches above the ground. It was not an altogether unpleasant sensation. And then he felt nothing at all.

The man with the rifle looked down impassively at the carnage. He sighed and rested the rifle across his shoulder and walked back to the horses. He rode carefully down the hill, holding the reins of the other three mounts, and his trail intersected the narrow-gauge tracks. A half-mile further, the engine sat patiently, steam drifting up into the cold. Luke Tate was waiting by the boxcar.

"Now, you didn't need to worry, did you?" the man said. "Worked just the way I said it would."

Tate tried to keep the shake out of his voice, but he was staring at the three horses. "Three of 'em?" The words almost stuck in his throat.

"Don't worry about it, Tate. They go to the railhead, same as the cattle. Just get the car open."

In moments, the three saddle horses joined the confused cattle. Tate slid the door closed. He couldn't meet the other man's even gaze. "Who . . . who were the others? Besides Taber?"

The man remounted his own horse and looked down. "Less you know, the better, mister. Move this train." He turned his horse and rode slowly back up the tracks. Tate watched him ride away until horse and rider were obscured by the newly falling snow. He shivered.

"Never again," he breathed. He turned and hurried down the length of the train to the cab where Scott waited. "Phillip, he killed three men!" Tate blurted out. "Ain't no money worth that." He grabbed the shovel and began to stoke the fire vigorously. "He's made us a part of it, Phillip. God Almighty, we're in on murder!" The two men looked at each other for a long moment. Then Scott hit the steam valve.

"We'll figure out what to do by the time we hit Littel," he said, but he couldn't keep the tremor out of his voice.

"We better think of something good," Tate said. "Anyone ever finds out, we'll hang, sure as hell."

XIII

BERT Schmidt reined in the Belgian and watched the children ahead of him. There were four, none older than ten. As far as he could tell, they were the only ones enjoying the aftermath of the blizzard. The four-foot drifts that choked Williams, clogged doorways, buried woodpiles and threatened, by sheer weight, to collapse roofs, became a playground.

The latest storm had begun on December 8. The line between sky and earth was lost. Cattle by the hundreds were pushed against fences and into small stands of brush or trees, where they huddled helplessly. Those that were strong enough survived. Hundreds did not.

The morning of December 11 dawned bright. The sun became a giant fireball that reflected from each diamond of moisture on the ground. Not a breath of wind stirred. As Schmidt rode down to the village, his cheeks tingled in the ten degree air. Wisps of smoke drifted up marking snug homes. The snow around the cabins was like a down quilt. If a man could afford to stay inside, he was all right. And that was one of Schmidt's troubles. Unless the weather stayed clear, it would be weeks before the men could begin logging again. Some would work at the mill, but others would have to wait for the cutting season in the spring. It was a decision he hated to make. In the dead of winter, there was little work anywhere. A few traveled to the cities, looking for the stray job. But most of them would stay on the mountain waiting.

He sat on the wide back of the Belgian and watched the children. One of them had a small wooden sled. They toiled up the hill that led to the Gilmore's, and then all four created

83

a shrieking, squirming bundle as they rode the sled down the hill. The sled ricocheted from hump to hump and finally deposited the youngsters at the bottom of the hill where they screamed with delight, each one a miniature snowman with fine powder clinging to his woolen clothes. Schmidt grinned and urged his horse toward the small cabin that nestled in the trees.

"I stopped by to see how your wood was holding out," he said when Carlotta Webster answered his knock.

She smiled and held the door open. "Come in out of the cold," she said. "I think you brought me considerably more than three weeks' worth."

Schmidt entered and stamped his feet. Now that he was inside, he didn't quite know what to say. "You making out all right?"

The woman nodded. "I made some gingerbread to celebrate the sunshine this morning. I think I would have died if it had been snowing again when I got up. When I saw the sunshine . . ." She smiled at Schmidt. "Would you like some while it's fresh?"

"Why, sure."

"And I bet you'd like coffee."

"Well, ah . . ."

"Of course you would." She went to the cupboard and got the pot. "I'll only be a moment." She went outside and scooped the pot full of clean snow and returned. When she set the pot on top of the stove, the snow clinging to the outside ran down and hissed on the hot cast iron. She glanced at Schmidt and blushed. "You know, I didn't take your good advice."

He looked perplexed.

"The rain barrel. I didn't empty it. It froze and burst."

"Lucky we got lots of snow, then," Schmidt said cheerfully. Carlotta smiled. He was pleased to see that her spirit had begun to mend.

"So you're making out all right," Schmidt said again. He watched her pour a handful of grounds into the pot.

"Milly Gilmore says that you have to think the bad things away." She glanced at Schmidt. "I've been trying to do that."

"Does it work?"

She cut the gingerbread expertly and put pieces on two tin plates. "I have all winter to work at it. Can you still find your sawmill in all this snow?"

"Just." Schmidt said as he chuckled.

She sat down and Schmidt noticed that there were only two chairs in the cabin, both simple wooden ladderbacks. "Why don't you take your coat off?" Carlotta asked. He jerked his hat and gloves off as if they were afire, and looked sheepish.

"Hate to get snow all over your floor," he said. He hung the coat on the doorlatch. He looked down at his boots and said, "Maybe I ought to shuck these."

"Don't be foolish. A little snow isn't going to hurt a thing. Rough as this floor is, you'll get splinters if you go barefoot. Have a seat Mister Schmidt." He settled gingerly into the straight chair. "Tell me about how your mill works."

"My mill?" He shrugged. "We just saw up trees. Make boards. You saw about all there is when you came up . . . ," he stopped in mid-sentence. The only time Carlotta Webster had been to the mill was when she'd come to kill him. Schmidt frowned. "I'm sorry. I didn't mean . . ."

"There's nothing to be sorry about." She stood and went to the stove and peered inside the coffee pot.

"As long as I brought it up, I might as well say it. I haven't heard anything, or found out anything, about your husband."

Carlotta watched the coffee grounds swirl in the near boiling water. She held the lid daintily in one hand, the hand poised a few inches above the pot as if ready to tap the lid in place should the water boil up. "I don't think we'll ever know," she said quietly. She replaced the lid and turned to look at Schmidt. "I don't think we'll ever know. As Milly Gilmore says, the Lord has a reason."

"You think a lot of her."

Carlotta nodded. "She is a very . . . strong woman. She's been a great help to me." She smiled at the lumberman. "And so have you. I'm finding I have friends I didn't know I had." She ran a hand through her hair and sighed. "I must owe Mister Buchanan a fortune. He just keeps saying, 'Don't worry none.' I'll pay him back, somehow. Come spring."

"I'm sure he means what he said."

"I won't have many friends if I become a beggar, you know."

"It's not begging. It's credit. You have to eat."

"I suppose so. I keep telling myself, come spring, everything will work out."

"And it will."

"I think the coffee is boiling, finally," she said. "I'll get some snow to settle the grounds." She went outside and returned with a small ball of fluffy snow and dropped it into the pot. When she poured a cupful, the coffee was dark and rich. "And here's your gingerbread," she said. Schmidt set the coffee cup on the floor and took the plate.

"You're not having coffee?"

She shook her head. "I hate coffee." She grinned at the astonishment on Schmidt's face. "I keep it for guests. Please . . . enjoy it." She watched him sip the coffee while he balanced the plate on his knee. "So, tell me, how long have you lived in Williams, Mister Schmidt?"

"I'd rather you called me Bert, ma'am. And I've been in these parts for fourteen years."

"I didn't think there were that many trees," she said. "And before that may I ask?"

"Minnesota."

"How did you ever happen to end up here?"

"You could ask that of anyone in town, ma'am, including

yourself." Schmidt blew on the steaming coffee, sipped, and winced.

"It's that bad?"

"Just hot."

"When the trees are all cut, where will you go?"

"I've been thinking . . ." Schmidt stopped. He'd never told anyone what he'd been thinking. "Maybe Vancouver."

"That's a far piece."

He smiled. "I have a train."

"Ah," she nodded. "That wonderful locomotive of yours." She grinned mischievously. "You must be very rich."

"Yep." They both laughed.

"I think I'm rather nosey."

"Perfectly all right, ma'am."

"Do you have any predictions about the weather?"

"It'll get worse. Everybody's saying it will. I have no reason to expect otherwise."

"If the snow gets so deep, how do you manage to cut down the trees, or pull them anywhere afterwards? I'd think it would be difficult."

Schmidt cupped the tin coffee mug between both hands and leaned forward. "That is an understatement. We don't cut in the dead of winter. We try to get it all over with so we can mill during the worst months."

"That sounds very practical."

Schmidt shrugged. "I don't believe in fighting things I can't lick."

"And it really pays to ship the lumber all that way? I mean, to build your own railroad and all?"

"It pays. A wagon's too slow, it carries too little. Down in the cities, there's always need for lumber. More than any of us can ever cut. I don't think it will end 'til every tree in the territory is gone."

Children's voices drifted over from the hill. "They're looking forward to Christmas," she said wistfully.

"We put on quite a feed come Christmas day up on the hill.

You think maybe you'd care to join us?" Schmidt asked. "A lot of womenfolk will be there. Turkey, all the fixings. There's always some singing, even move the tables out of the way and dance a bit."

"I didn't know you were a cook as well."

"I'm not," Schmidt said quickly. "I got me two of the best French Canadian cooks a man could want. What do you say?"

Carlotta looked at him, and Schmidt found himself staring helplessly into her eyes.

"I'd like that very much."

Schmidt slapped his knee. "Good. Good. We eat along about two o'clock. 'Course, you're welcome any time before that. How about if I send down a wagon?"

"It's such a short distance, I think I can manage. After all, I did once before." This time, she said it and smiled.

A few minutes later Bert Schmidt leaned against the Belgian's saddle before mounting and said out loud, "By God, I'm courting the lady."

He rode the Belgian down the snow-packed street to the emporium. There was hardly room, with the snow drifts, to tie the horse to the nearly buried hitching rail but Schmidt was in too good a mood to cuss the snow. He went up the slippery steps, stamped his boots, and entered Buchanan's store. A clerk greeted Schmidt with a bright smile.

"Morning, Henny," Schmidt said cheerfully. He slapped his gloves together.

Henrietta McDowell, pudgy, short, and efficient, came around the end of the counter. "Mercy," she said, "I would have thought that you'd be snowed in on that hill until Easter."

"Not as bad as all that."

"What can I help you with this morning, then?"

Schmidt moved to the display of clothing, and critically eyed the selection. "I was kinda thinking that I'd like me a Christmas shirt."

Henrietta smiled. "A Christmas shirt."

"Yup. Something special." He lifted corners of fabric and inspected the ends of bolts.

"Ready made?"

He grinned. "I'm not much for sewing. Unless you want to do it . . ."

"Been done before," Henrietta said. "But look at these now." She lifted a small pile of shirts, carefully folded. "Milly Gilmore makes these. Look at this stitchery."

"Milly does that?" Schmidt wasn't sure what he was supposed to be looking at.

"Yes, sir, she does. Couldn't find better. Now, look here." She leaned over, her substantial bosom threatening to dislodge another pile of clothing. "This, Mister Schmidt, is a Christmas shirt." She pulled out the garment and unfolded it. She held the shirt by the shoulders so Schmidt could see it in all its red, black, and green glory. "It's wool, too," she added, as if that clinched it. Schmidt eyed the bright checkered pattern thoughtfully. "And I think it will fit." She smiled. "If it doesn't, we'll make it fit!"

"You think so?"

"Try it on. Just take it back there in the stockroom and see how nice you look."

Schmidt nodded. Within minutes, he was rubbing his rough hands down the downy sleeves, admiring the texture. The fit was good. He stepped back into the store and Henrietta nodded appreciatively.

"Now, don't you look fine?" she asked, and Schmidt grinned happily and retreated to the stockroom. When he emerged again in his old clothes, he felt shabby.

"I'll take it," he said.

Henrietta lay the shirt on the counter and patted the fabric. "You have a decent pair of trousers to set all this off?"

"Well . . ."

"I know you folks up at the mill. Never see you without some grease from that darn machinery on you." She smiled and laid a hand on Schmidt's arm. "I talk with Alice now and then. She says the same thing about Jean-Paul. He has one decent pair of Sunday trousers, and that's it."

"Seems like that ought to be enough."

"Men," Henrietta scoffed.

"Well, show me what you got, then." Before Schmidt was ready to leave, he had purchased not only a pair of new trousers but a pair of brown dress boots as well.

As she tallied the purchases, she said, "Now, you're ready, young man."

"Been a while since I've been called that," Schmidt remarked. As he pulled out his money, something caught his eye. He stepped over and looked down at the scarves.

"Milly makes those, too. Best lady with knitting needles I've ever seen. Wool comes from that place down south. Milly buys the darkest fleeces, and spins it up. Just feel that." She picked up the top scarf. It was a deep, rich brown with flecks of white and gray in the wool.

"I'll take that too," he said.

"Something the matter?"

Schmidt shifted a foot, embarrassed. "If you was to buy a pair of gloves for a lady, how would you go about it? I mean, you have something like that here?"

"Certainly. Right over here." Henrietta didn't seem to think the request out of the ordinary at all and Schmidt was relieved. "How large are her hands?"

"Uh . . ."

"Is she as large as me?"

"Uh . . ." Schmidt eyed Henrietta's ample bulk.

"I mean is she as tall as me."

"Yes. Just about. But, uh . . ."

"Not so fat?"

Schmidt smiled at Henrietta's engaging honesty. "She's a little skinnier than you."

She bustled over to the gloves. "Something warm, or something fancy?"

"Both."

Schmidt purchased two pairs. As he got ready to leave, he was stopped by a booming voice.

"Bert!" Mike Buchanan shouted from the doorway that led into the emporium's café and saloon. "I've been looking for you."

"Well, here I am. I've about made you all the money you'll need for the winter."

Buchanan looked at the bundles and grinned. "Keep it up. Keep it up." He walked in and leaned on the counter beside Henrietta and looked at Bert. "Ain't seen you in a coon's age. I've been runnin' around, you've been runnin' around, and now this storm." He shook his head in exasperation. "Can we work a deal on the ice again this year."

Schmidt put the bundles down. "Don't see why not."

"Way I figure it, with this cold weather, Tulley Lake is froze as deep as I need it. If I could have about six of your men and three of your sleds . . ."

"Yep. I don't give much chance that you can get in the Tulley Lake trail until some of the snow melts, though. Not much traffic up that way. Snow's not packed. Hell on horses."

"Oh, hell, yes. I don't let a few little drifts stand in my way. Run through there about twice with a good team and a heavy cutter, and it'll be easy as you please."

"When do you want them?"

"Well," and Buchanan tapped the counter. "I'd like to get that ice before there's much more snow blows in on the lake. And I think we're going to get more. You pulled your men out of the timber yet?"

Schmidt nodded.

"Well, then. How about let's try Monday? Six men, the three cutters, saws, the whole works."

Schmidt smiled and nodded at the bundles. "Be my chance to get back at you for all this."

"I was afraid of that."

"You going to want more coal?"

Buchanan shook his head. "Got all I think I'll need. Could be wrong, might be cussing myself in March, but I think I'm set."

"Well, if you change your mind, just holler. Train'll be running just about every two weeks. Easy as not to take the boxcar down, too. Won't if I don't need to. So let me know."

"I'll do that. Don't forget Monday, now," Buchanan said as Schmidt gathered up his purchases. Schmidt tied the packages behind the saddle and rode out of Williams. The mill came into view and Schmidt frowned. Seven horses, five with riders still mounted, were standing in the snow in front of the main building. He kicked the Belgian into a faster walk. He saw the bulky figure of Jean-Paul Gingras. The foreman was talking with two of the riders. One he didn't recognize. But as he rode closer, he saw the other was Sam Averill of the Triple S ranch.

XIV

"MISTER Schmidt, I think we'd best have us a talk," Sam Averill said. Schmidt looked at Gingras. The Frenchman's face was sober.

"Fair enough," Schmidt replied. He twisted in his saddle and looked at the men from the Triple S. They were a tough, hardy bunch. Their faces were grim. "No point in us standing out here in the cold. Tell you what, Jean-Paul, why don't you show these fellas where the chowhall is. I expect they took little pleasure in that long ride up here this morning. Have Juteau fix up some coffee. Averill, we'll ride over to my cabin. It's just through the trees over there." He nodded to the east. "Then we can talk."

"We didn't come for your hospitality," Averill snapped.

Schmidt leaned forward and crossed his forearms over the saddlehorn. "No, you didn't. And I can guess what's on your mind. But you've ridden the better part of thirty miles, and that means you left before sunup. Now, you can have your men sit out here in the cold, as you like. Me, I'm riding over to the cabin. You want to speak with me, you come along. Jean-Paul, show these men where the chowhall is. If they want to wait outside, that's their concern." Without waiting for a reply, he kicked the Belgian and the big horse stepped out, leaving the men behind.

The men looked at Averill uncertainly. The rancher's face was dark. "Go with him," he said shortly, jerking his head at Gingras. The rancher swung up on his horse and trotted after Schmidt.

Inside the cabin, Schmidt put his purchases down and checked the stove. He threw a scuttlefull of knots in and

93

clanged the door shut. Averill entered without knocking and stood by the door, watching him. Schmidt put the coffee pot on the top plate of the stove, then took off his heavy coat and gloves.

"What's on your mind?" Schmidt asked. Averill relaxed enough to take off his own gloves.

"Where's Taber?" Averill asked.

"He works for you, not me."

Averill's eyes narrowed. "I want a straight answer."

The stove was beginning to roar and Schmidt tapped the lower damper a little. "Averill, your range detective is a sore point with me. I've no doubt that he's reported to you about what happened here. The less I see of him, the better. He was here when O. B. Webster got shot. He knows I didn't do it, but he shoved a gun in my face anyway. He left here a little the worse for wear." Schmidt stood with his hands resting lightly on his hips. "I don't see it as my job to keep track of the men you hire."

"He and two of my men rode out of the Triple S Sunday. I haven't heard from them since."

"Where were they headed?"

"You know that as well as I do."

Schmidt sighed. "Averill, I'm not one for puzzles. Speak your mind."

"All right. I'll play it your way. Taber told me that he had evidence that some of my cattle were being shipped down to the railroad on your locomotive."

Dead silence filled the cabin as the two men stood and faced each other. "And?" Schmidt said quietly.

Averill slowly unbuttoned his coat. The cabin was warm, but that wasn't what prompted his move.

"He wanted to ride here with two of my men. I sent my foreman, Tom Burke. Borden Payne went along. That was Sunday. I didn't think much about it. I got me worries enough right now with this weather. Haven't seen them since. Tom Burke's got a young wife who's with child."

Schmidt turned and found himself a cup. "Coffee?" Averill shook his head. Schmidt poured thoughtfully, then set the pot back on the stove. "They might have holed up somewhere."

"Storm's been spent for more'n a day. They would have showed. I rode up to find 'em."

"Averill, you know this country as well as me. If those men were caught in the open range during a storm, they're most likely froze to death. I can tell you two things. They didn't show here. I was down in the village this morning. I didn't hear any word there. No one I saw was talking about seeing your men." He looked at the rancher. "This man Taber's held me a grudge since a month ago, when I beat him, and beat him bad. He was onto something. The man he was following, Webster, tried to sell me beef. Maybe it was yours. Taber said it was. I'm sure he told you all about it."

"Taber told me you set Webster up to be killed."

"Taber's a liar. Someone shot O. B. Webster, all right. Slugs came out of the dark, from over in the timber. We never saw the rifle flashes. I'll tell you this . . . if someone's taking your beef, it isn't me. I don't much like being accused of that. I got problems enough of my own."

Averill met Schmidt's level gaze, then looked down at the floor and sighed. He was at a loss.

"If I was you, I'd set my mind to finding those men. You do that, maybe Taber will have some answers. I tell you straight that cattle rustling is not my business. I think you know that. If Taber says it is, then I want to talk to him as bad as you. He told you he was riding up this way? Fine. He's not here. You're free to look around the mill all you like. If you're concerned about my engine, it's over under the shed roof. Help yourself."

Averill looked grim. "We already did . . . or started to. We looked some, until your foreman came boiling out of the mill. About that time, you showed up."

"I'm glad I did, then. Gingras is a good man."

"Didn't seem to bother him much that there was seven of us."

"It wouldn't. Not him. All I can say is that if Taber had some bee in his bonnet about my train, you best ride back by way of the tracks. Maybe you'll find something."

"That's the way we rode up."

"And found nothing?"

"Not a thing."

Schmidt shrugged and set down his empty cup. "Then I don't know what to tell you. It's a big country, Averill. You want some of my men to help you search, I can give you fifteen, maybe twenty. With this snow, I've pulled the crews out of the deep timber. And there's more winter on the way, you can bet on that. You don't have much time."

Averill thrust his hands in his pockets. "Mister Schmidt, I've heard you're a fair and a reasonable man. I have no reason not to believe that. Taber was onto something, but he's a close-mouthed son of a bitch. I should have taken the time to find out more, but I didn't. Maybe the three of 'em are already back at the Triple S. Maybe we crossed trails somewhere. But there's too many miles of range for us to search, not knowing what to look for."

"If I was you, I'd take a meal at the chowhall and ride back to the ranch, before this weather turns. Search again along the tracks, and later, if my men find anything, you'll be the first to know."

For the first time since his arrival, Averill smiled. He nodded slowly. "Takes a man with a right strong backbone to stand being accused of rustling and then offer hospitality."

"You didn't accuse me of rustling," Schmidt said easily. He reached for his coat. "Taber did. If it'd been any other way, you wouldn't be standing there now." Averill's eyebrows shot up and Schmidt nodded at the door. "Let's fetch something to eat."

When Sam Averill and his men left the mill, Averill made a point of shaking hands with both Schmidt and Gingras. The six men with Averill were well fed, if puzzled by the turn of events. They had ridden the better part of thirty miles, spoiling for a fight, and the cold hours in the saddle hadn't dulled their anger any. Instead of a fight, they had been offered chuck. They had seen Averill walk into the chowhall with Schmidt and read nothing on their boss's face but impatience. When they all rode out, they heard Sam Averill say, as he leaned down to shake hands, "Mister Schmidt, I'm in your debt. I hope it stays that way."

As the Triple S men rode out, Schmidt rested a hand on Gingras's shoulder. The two men walked toward the mill.

"Jean-Paul, I feel like a goddamned blind man. Suppose this Taber bastard is speaking a grain of truth. Suppose that." He stopped and faced his mill foreman, a man whom he trusted implicitly. "Is there any way you can think of, any way at all, that my locomotive could be used by someone to ship rustled cattle? Right under my blind nose?"

"Of course," Gingras said without hesitation, "they could stop the train out on the prairie somewhere and herd the cattle on board. The boxcar is the only way. But . . ." he hesitated, looking sideways at Schmidt. "How many would that car hold? And they could be seen by anyone. Anyone at all, who might be riding by."

"Like Taber. He told Averill he had some evidence. The only way he could have evidence is if he saw something. And if the train was being used, then my engineer would know about it."

Gingras frowned. "He would have to, Bert." He looked pained as he added, "So would Tate. For that matter, the station agent at the railhead would have to know. Dick Smith. He would have to know."

Schmidt and Gingras stood still, halfway between the chowhall and the mill. After a long moment's silence, Schmidt said quietly, "It is possible, then, isn't it? Taber could be right."

"Perhaps."

"Why would he have ridden this way with two other men?

If he was after me, he would come by himself. He did, last week. Asked me about the train, now that I think about it. For God's sake, you saw him too. You were the one who told me he was here. He said he'd come to apologize for what he did. I didn't believe what he was saying then, and I still don't. Sam Averill says Taber and the two cowpunchers left the Triple S last Sunday. That was after Taber was here to talk to me. He must have been trying to find something out."

"It is simple then," Gingras said. "Talk to Tate and Scott. A man may lie with words, mon ami, but his face, his eyes . . . that is something else. You want me to talk with them?"

Schmidt stood silently, lost in thought. "No. I'll take care of it. I'm not about to accuse two of my best men on the say-so of a bastard like Taber. Something's going on, Jean-Paul. I've been sitting on my ass, ignoring it. I guess it's time I took Taber a little more seriously. Don't say anything to any of the men. If they ask about Averill's visit today, just say they're looking for some men they think got lost in the storm. That'll be the truth."

"As you like. If there is anything else I can do . . ."

"Thanks. Just keep the lumber coming out the ass end of that mill." The noon whistle shrieked and the saws wound down. "I'll talk with you this afternoon." Men began to emerge from the mill and Schmidt found himself scrutinizing their faces.

He entered the mill but passed directly through, through the drifts toward the shed where the locomotive sat, polished and waiting. He walked the engine's length, and after he had passed along two of the flatcars, he saw the tracks in the snow where Averill and his men had first encountered Jean-Paul. He wondered briefly what the Frenchman had told them. Schmidt walked on, once stumbling in a deep drift. He caught his balance by laying a hand on the wooden side of the boxcar. He reached the rear of the train, crossed the tracks, and forced open the boxcar doors with a grunt. Snow was frozen in the tracks of the door, and it moved stiffly. He looked into the dark interior of the car. Light filtered through the cracks in its wooden sides and Schmidt pushed both doors fully open. Then he swung himself up into the car and began a methodical scrutiny of its musty insides.

It took only moments before his sharp eyes found something that made his stomach knot and his pulse race. In a dark corner, perhaps three feet off the floor, a tuft of coarse hair was caught in a splinter of one of the siding boards. Schmidt pulled it loose and stepped into the light to examine it. He fluffed it with his gloved fingers. The muscles around his jaws tightened. Holding the tuft in one hand, he resumed his inspection. By the time he finished, fifteen minutes later, he had five more similar tufts. And, caught in the cracks between several of the floorboards was enough residue of cattle manure that any doubt Schmidt may have had finally vanished. The car was clean, but not clean enough.

"Son of a bitch," he muttered. "How the hell did they figure to get away with it?" Anger welled up in him like a tide. He pounded his gloved fist against the side of the car. He leaped down into the snow and set off toward the chowhall, savagely kicking through the snow, head pulled down into his collar. His fists, one of them still full of the bits of manure and hide, were balled at his sides.

XV

A DOZEN or more mouths, most full of food, gaped with astonishment as Bert Schmidt burst through the door of the chowhall. He stood for only a second as his eyes adjusted to the dim light of the hall. Jean-Paul Gingras rose to his feet, the only man in the hall who knew the cause of his employer's wrath. As he rose, his eyes turned and found Luke Tate and Phillip Scott. The two engineers were sitting together in a knot of men near the kitchen end of the hall. Bert Schmidt strode over to their table and glared down at the two astonished men. Their faces drained of color. The hall fell silent. Smooth as a cat, Gingras left his seat and approached the men. Tate turned, saw Gingras, and paled even more. He swiveled in panic to gape at Schmidt.

"What's . . ." Scott started to say.

Schmidt opened his glove and tossed the hair and manure into the remains of Scott's mincemeat pie. His hands hung at his sides, but they shook with fury. "Before I turn you over to Sam Averill, there's two things you'd better tell me, you miserable son of a bitch." Schmidt leaned forward and rested his hands on the table. He ignored the man who pushed his chair aside to clear Schmidt's path. His men had not seen Schmidt in a rage often, but after the first few times, they'd learned to blend with the woodwork. Schmidt's eyes locked with Scott's. "I want to know who you're working for, shipping those cattle of Averill's?" He paused. Scott closed his mouth and swallowed. Bert Schmidt's voice dropped to a whisper. "And then, you'll tell me where those three men are."

"Three men?" Scott quavered.

"Taber. Burke. Payne." Schmidt spat out the three names and then slammed his fist on the table so hard the tin plates danced. "Where are they, mister!" he shouted. "And don't tell me you don't know. It's written all over your sorry faces!" He leaned forward even further and glared first at Scott and then at Tate. "I don't care how you did it, but by God you'll tell me where those men are."

Luke Tate let out a cry and shot to his feet, his chair flying backwards. Gingras, looming behind him, reacted just as fast. He grabbed Tate by one arm but the man's strength grew in proportion to his panic. He jerked free, staggered backward, and nearly fell. Eyes wild, he lunged toward the table and grabbed the large knife that was skewered deep in a loaf of brown bread. The knife came clear as chunks of the loaf scattered across the table. Gingras waded in, searching for an opening. The other mill hands ducked. Tate slashed and the point of the knife caught in the heavy sleeve of Gingras's shirt. The foreman swept a hand that knocked Tate onto the table. Dishes and metalware scattered, and Tate rolled away. In the split second that Tate's back was turned, Gingras grabbed him by both shoulders. The big Frenchman twisted, intending to pitch Tate toward the wall where he could be pinned, but Tate lashed out wildly. The knife slashed by Gingras's face. Tate's wrist struck the foreman in the mouth and his grip loosened.

Tate scrambled away. The knife flew out of his hand and skittered on the floor, but he dove for it and clutched the handle, coming up in a crouch.

"Leave it be, Tate," Schmidt snapped. He moved to block the doorway when he saw Tate's eyes shift in that direction. Jean-Paul Gingras was in no mood to outwait the man. He stormed around the end of the table. Spittle flew from Tate's mouth as he yelled and lunged with the knife. Gingras's hand clamped on the man's wrist and the two crashed into each other, careening into the corner.

Bert Schmidt moved equally fast. He grabbed a two-foot

length of split pine from the neat pile by the stove. When he swung, he swung to kill. The firewood cracked Tate's skull with a dull, ugly sound, and the man collapsed, his fingers releasing the knife. Gingras pulled free and got to his feet.

"Mother of God," one of the loggers said. Bert Schmidt looked down in disgust at the body, then turned. His gaze traveled down the length of the hall and rested on Phillip Scott. Scott came slowly to his feet.

"I ain't goin' nowhere," he said softly. Both Schmidt and Gingras advanced on him, but he held his ground.

It was Schmidt who spoke first. "The rest of you men get out of here," he said. He didn't say it loudly, but no one stayed long enough to be told twice.

"I'll tell you what I know," Scott said. He looked with apprehension at the glowering Gingras, then back at Schmidt.

"Damned right you will," Schmidt said. "Sit down. Let's hear it."

Scott collapsed in the chair, and sat with his head in his hands. He could not bring himself to look down the hall at his dead partner. He told the whole story, and not once did he look up to meet Schmidt's gaze. When he finished, Schmidt sat back and looked at his foreman.

"What do you think?"

Gingras shrugged. "Possible."

Schmidt eyed the engineer thoughtfully. Scott still sat with his head in his hands, staring dumbly at the table top. "You realize what you're accusing Mike Buchanan of?" Schmidt asked quietly.

"Yes."

"Not just rustling, Scott. You say he's guilty of murder. Not once. Four times. Webster, Taber, Burke, Payne. You're saying Mike Buchanan killed all those men."

"Yes."

"And cold-blooded as hell."

For the first time since he had begun his confession, Phillip

Scott lifted his head and looked full at Bert Schmidt. "I'm not just sayin' it, boss. I know it for a fact. Like I said, me and Luke . . ." His voice broke and quickly recovered. "Me and Luke heard those shots after the cattle was loaded. Buchanan came back down the hill with the horses. I knew what he did." He wiped his face with one hand. "I know it don't make no difference, but me and Luke had decided after that we was goin' to have nothin' to do with Buchanan no more."

"A little late."

Scott nodded and put his head back in his hands.

"How much did he pay you?"

It was a long time before the answer came, but finally Scott said, "He paid me and Luke five hundred dollars."

"Five hundred dollars for each trip?"

Scott shook his head. "No. Five hundred. One time. So he could use the boxcar any time he had cattle."

"How many times did you make the run with cattle?" Schmidt asked, incredulous.

"Twice this year. Did it four times last year. Couple times before that. Lot of times it was butchered beef, not livestock at all. Nothing like this ever happened."

"What was Webster's part? Do you know?"

Scott looked up again. "He ran cattle once in a while. But from what I hear, he wasn't no good on a horse. Buchanan used him to get beef for the ice house."

"Ice house?"

"Yep. Buchanan said he took a few head now and then, butchered 'em, kept the beef to sell in his café. You dig under some of that sawdust in that ice house, and you'll find more'n ice, boss."

"Jean-Paul, that explains where Webster got that beef the night he came up to my cabin. Why'd he come to me?"

"Taber caught him red-handed," Scott said. "Webster figured maybe, by blamin' you, he'd have time to get back to Buchanan and tell him about Taber. Webster, he used to work for you, 'til he got fired. I guess your name just come to mind. Taber thought Webster was telling the truth. For a while, anyways. Then, I guess he didn't know what to think." He looked briefly at Schmidt. "I only talked to Buchanan about it once, real quick like. He seemed to think it was pretty funny. He said that no matter what Webster said about you, nobody'd ever believe it."

"So, to keep him from talking any more, Buchanan shot him on my doorstep." Scott nodded. "And the men who corraled the cattle. You say there were two of them?"

"Yes."

"Just drifters?"

"Yes. Worked off and on for Dick Smith, down at the railhead." Scott smiled grimly. "I don't guess you'll be seein' them in the territory again."

"So of this gang," Gingras said slowly, "the only ones left are Buchanan, you, and this Dick Smith? You didn't work with anyone else from the mill?" He reached forward and grabbed Scott by the shirt front. "Who is running down the hill right now to tell Buchanan?"

"There ain't nobody else," Scott said.

"You and Tate were the only ones from here?" Schmidt persisted.

"Yes." Scott glanced up at Schmidt. "Unless Tate got down there just a bit ago, Buchanan don't know about Averill comin' up here, or you findin' out."

Schmidt's eyes narrowed. "Tate was down in the village?"

"I ain't sayin' he was. But he coulda been. When Averill and his men come up the hill . . . well, from then on to when we come in here, I don't know. I didn't see him. He coulda been, is all I'm sayin'."

Gingras stood up. "Then Buchanan may already be gone."

"Get your rifle," Schmidt said. "D'Arlene!" The French cook was standing in the kitchen doorway. "Make sure this man stays here." He jerked a thumb at Scott. "And have Pierre find two men to cairn Tate's body."

Moments later, the two men were plunging down the hill

toward Williams. Once in the village, they skirted behind the buildings, passing by the ice house. Pressing close to the wall of the emporium, Schmidt reached the back door. He held a Colt revolver in one hand and reached for the latch with the other. The door opened easily. As soon as it did, the normal sounds of the emporium's saloon drifted out. Schmidt frowned, listening intently. Holding the gun down beside his leg, he slipped through the door with Gingras immediately behind them. The stockroom led directly into the saloon proper. Schmidt waited a moment for his eyes to adjust to the dim light, and then moved forward. One of Buchanan's girls was working in the saloon, and there were seven customers. But there was no Mike Buchanan. Ignoring the puzzled looks, Schmidt strode through the saloon and entered the dry goods store. Henrietta McDowell was behind the counter. She looked up and saw the two loggers, and then saw the guns.

"Mister Schmidt, what . . ."

"Where's Mike Buchanan?" Schmidt said sharply.

"Well, I don't know where Mr. Buchanan is," the stout woman replied. "Now just what is going on?"

"Nothing you need to worry about, ma'am. It's Mike I need. You have no idea . . ."

"All I know is that he was rummaging around here in a sweat about an hour ago." Mrs. McDowell waved a hand. "But isn't he always? I ignored him. There's a lot to do here, you know. Mercy me, I have no idea."

"No idea where he went? Or when he plans to come back?"

"When he was in here, he muttered something about Tully Lake, but I ignored him because I had a customer at the time."

"You have no idea what he took with him?" Schmidt asked.

"I didn't pay any attention. But if I see him, I'll let him know you want to speak with him."

Schmidt was about to leave when he stopped. "Do you know if he took one of the horses?"

"Oh, indeed," Mrs. McDowell replied. "He dropped the saddle back there in the stockroom. As you probably know, Mr. Buchanan is capable of cussing at times." She smiled faintly. "He did then. My customer was Mrs. Gilmore. Most embarrassing." She looked again at Gingras's rifle and the handgun Schmidt held. "I hope there's been no trouble up at the mill."

"Nothing to worry about," Schmidt said, and then he and Gingras hurried out. They plowed through the snow that had drifted beside the emporium and made their way to the small stock shed and corral on the east side of the building. Schmidt stood for a moment, thoughtful. "The only horse I know for sure that he owns is that big gray. The one with the fancy dappled rump." He pointed with the Colt. "He's not there."

"There are not so many places he could go, the weather like this," Gingras said.

"Nope." Schmidt thrust the handgun into his coat pocket. "He said Tully, but it's my guess he said that for Mrs. McDowell's benefit. There's nothing up that way. Past Tully it's deep timber. East and west is open range. He'd be a fool to strike out either way."

"That leaves south . . . the railhead," Gingras said.

"That's right. He'd go that way. Warn Smith. Wouldn't be long before there'd be a mainliner he could board." Schmidt was already in motion, pushing through the snow toward the main street of Williams.

"He would leave all of this?" Gingras said, indicating the emporium."

"Hell yes. And I'll bet you that if a man was to search the place, the only money left would be the change Henrietta has in the dry goods store, and the little that Mona has in the saloon. My guess is Mike would clear out as quick as he could. If we can get to the railhead before he does, maybe we have a chance. Averill's men have already broken the snow for him. That big gray won't have any trouble for the first half of the trip—until he reaches the point where Averill and his men swing west toward the ranch. Then he'll be breakin' snow where the wind hasn't swept clear. That's where we'll nail his hide."

XVI

NEVER had the steam boiler of the locomotive seemed so stubborn. Scott, pale and silent, stoked the firebox skillfully while Gingras and Schmidt tended to the horses. The three nervous animals were coaxed into the boxcar. They were work horses, hardly built for speed. But they would be more welcome than traveling on foot if the men had to leave the train. The Belgian, normally so even tempered, would have no part of the darkness of the car, nor of the narrow ramp. Finally, with a stout rope around his wide haunches and a resounding whack on the rump, he lunged up and in. His movements rocked the car.

Finally, at twenty minutes after two on the afternoon of December 11, 1886, Scott tapped a single, small note from the engine's steam whistle. In an instant, Schmidt and Gingras were in the cab. Schmidt figured the men from the Triple S had a two hour head start. Buchanan would be an hour behind them if Schmidt had read his intentions correctly. There was little chance the train would catch up with him before the Triple S cutoff.

Schmidt looked ahead through the narrow window. The rails were invisible under the snow, but the tracks of the horses were obvious, sometimes fanned out in several trails, sometimes cutting one narrow canyon through a drift three or four feet deep. The locomotive's cowcatcher shunted the snow aside easily, but Scott refused to edge the steam throttle forward. The possibility of derailment was more than an even bet. But Phillip Scott knew the engine and knew the roadbed. He jockeyed the locomotive down the mountain, easing it around the tortuous bends, and along the snakes of track that wound under the snow-bent crowns of blackjacks.

It would have been safer and faster to have left the four flatcars behind and trail only the tender and boxcar. But Schmidt had never built a siding at the mill. Short of tipping them off the tracks, there was no way to remove the flatcars and pull only the boxcar.

The train wound around the end of a bluff, and Scott's hands flew as he brought the train to a jarring, squealing stop.

"Shit," Schmidt cursed. He swung down out of the small cab and sank nearly to his knees in the snow. Fifty feet ahead, a razor-topped drift had blown diagonally across the tracks. The men could see where the riders had spurred their mounts down off the railbed, cutting around the deepest snow. On the tracks, the whitecap was even with Schmidt's head. He turned. "You can't break through?" Even before Scott could answer, Schmidt was floundering back to the engine.

"Toss me down the shovel from the tender," he shouted. "And if there's another one back in the boxcar, go get it." He attacked the center of the drift savagely, driving the shovel in deep and wrenching the snow downhill. Schmidt had no idea how much snowpack on the tracks the engine could cut. More on the downhill than up, maybe, where traction wasn't an issue, he thought. He shoveled down until the tool clanged against the rail, then started another swath. By that time, Gingras was at his elbow.

"Give it to me for a moment," the big Frenchman said, taking the shovel. Schmidt stood, his breath coming in gasps, while Gingras worked.

"Remind me to hang a couple shovels in that boxcar next time," he said. Gingras didn't bother with a reply. The bottom of the drift was perhaps twelve feet wide, and in another ten minutes the two men had carved out a narrow passageway for the engine. Schmidt waved at Scott and the engine hissed forward. The next mile of track lay across the high brow of a west-facing hill, a long, gentle slope of track that was unprotected from the wind.

The next drift was four feet high and covered nearly twenty feet of track. Schmidt dropped down again into the snow, kicking the powder with his boots. "Real slow," he shouted at Scott, and then bent down at the edge of the drift near the tracks, watching the engine ease forward. The spade of the cowcatcher dug into the snow until the drift formed a bow wave across the lower front of the boiler. Schmidt beckoned forward with his hand. He knelt low, face only inches from the front idlers and the drive wheel. Abruptly he chopped with his hand and the drive wheel locked. He stood up, beckoning for the shovel. "Go any further and it'll pack right up off the rails," he said. And he and Gingras dug through that drift, and another, and another, chopping passage through five before they reached the protection of the trees at the corner, a mile and a half below the mill. At that point, the track turned sharply and ran downhill due west, and most of that way, the tracks were swept clear.

Three miles south of the mill, another drift, approachable if the men were gamblers, blocked the tracks. Gingras was down off the engine before it had groaned to a stop. For perhaps a minute, he dug furiously, and then Schmidt touched his arm. "Wait a minute."

"What?"

"Listen . . ." They stood quietly, breath gently steaming. Off through the timber to the south, Schmidt pointed, head cocked. "There, again." The gunshot was flat and without echo. Three more followed, and then several more. Gingras drove the shovel in a fury then, and in moments the locomotive was underway again.

"How far ahead, do you guess?" the Frenchman asked.

"Mile, maybe two. Maybe more. It's hard to figure," Schmidt shouted. He pulled his head inside. "A man could push a horse pretty good in this, deep as the drifts are. Most places it's blown clear, or you can ride around the worst of them." **He** shrugged.

"You figure it's him?" Scott yelled over the sounds of the engine.

"I figure he's one of them," Schmidt replied. He picked up the rifle. "And I'd give a lot to know who else. If it's Averill and his men, either they rode awful slow so that Buchanan caught up with 'em, or they doubled back for some reason." He handed Gingras the rifle, and drew out his revolver. He rapped the barrel against the wood of the cab. "Keep your eyes open. This won't stop any bullets."

When Sam Averill and his six ranch hands left the mill, they didn't tarry. It was noon, and the Triple S lay several hours to the southwest. Even if they were lucky and hit long stretches of prairie that were blown clear, they would ride the last hour or more in the dark. If it stayed clear, they could count on seeing the faint flicker of the Triple S kerosene lanterns far in the distance, while off to their left would be the rising shadow of Thunder Butte. If it didn't stay clear . . . Averill shuddered at the thought. He'd spent a night or two under a buffalo robe in his youth, while the wind whistled and the horses cringed with heads down and backs into the wind and snow. He didn't want to do it again.

Still, a worry far greater than the weather, the ride, or the not-too-distant nightfall nagged. Somewhere along the narrow-gauge track, Taber had said, rustlers were loading cattle onto Schmidt's train. The range detective had described a holding pen, a corral of sorts. If that was the case, it made sense that the corral was not out on the open prairie.

And so the seven men rode down the tracks, squinting against the glare of the snow. Billy Wentworth saw the sign and almost ignored it. The hills were starting to level out, and off to the right of the tracks, almost hidden behind the boulders, was the butt end of a four inch diameter pine pole.

Wentworth broke out from the line of horses and rode over to it. As soon as he reached the rocks, he was looking into the small canyon that Taber had discovered.

Averill rested his hands on his saddlehorn and looked up the canyon. He nodded as Wentworth held up the pine pole, its ends cut cleanly. "If this here's the spot Taber was talkin' about . . . makes sense to me that it is . . . then we're close to where he was plannin' to wait for the rustlers." He pulled his greatcoat up and fumbled out a pocket watch. After a glance at the time and then a look up at the still clear sky, he said, "Now here's what I want. If this is the spot, then maybe we'll find something. I want two of you to scout this ridge," he said and indicated behind the canyon, "and two of you over there. Me and Billy here and Joey will see about that rise over across the tracks."

As the bullets from the Winchester rifle had smashed Cyrus Taber to his death, his right hand had clawed up as if it could stop the slugs. It was that gloved hand half above the snow that was Billy Wentworth's second major find of the afternoon. He didn't have the stomach to pull on the hand, but Sam Averill did, and then the men from the Triple S were looking down at the frozen body. The rancher scowled as he brushed snow away and saw the four holes punched through the smooth sheepskin of Taber's coat. "Find the others," he said shortly. The seven men had little difficulty finishing the grim search, and when the bodies were laid out side by side, the cowpunchers waited for Averill to speak. The rancher held up Payne's buffalo gun. He levered the action open and drew out the big cartridge. "Never fired," he said. "And Tom never got his gun out of the holster." He knelt down and slipped his right glove off. With his face set in a grimace, he brushed the snow from the front of Payne's coat. "Look here." And it was easy to see. One frozen, gloved hand still gripped the center of the coat in a crumpled death hold. Above that was a black-ringed, burned hole. "Some bastard was standin' right close," he said softly. "Point blank."

He knelt for another minute, then stood up abruptly. "Billy, you and Milt and Joey are going to have to carry 'em on your horses. You're all light, and your mounts will take it as far as Williams."

"We're goin' back there, then?" one of the ranch hands asked.

"Yeah. We're goin' back."

XVII

AS his big gray followed the well-broken trail left by the seven Triple S riders, Mike Buchanan was relieved that he was traveling light. He was smart enough to know that time was his most valuable ally. With that in mind, he had fled Williams with all the cash he had hidden under the sawdust in the icehouse. That filled one side of the heavy saddlebags. In the other side were five boxes of .44 caliber ammunition that fit both his carbine and revolver. He had jammed a few articles of clothing and a quantity of beef jerky into a tightly rolled buffalo hide and strapped that tightly behind the saddle. The Winchester carbine went into the saddleboot. Under the ties that secured the buffalo hide he slid a four foot crowbar.

He rode out of Williams, his gut tight with tension. He hated to leave the emporium since there was so much more money to be made there. But, in the saddlebags, he carried enough for a first class start anywhere else in the country. As he swung south to follow the tracks, staying well clear of the mill, he glanced in that direction. Bert Schmidt was a bulldog. If Tate hadn't run down and tipped him off about Averill, he wouldn't have had a chance, Buchanan thought. Odds were that Schmidt had already checked the emporium. He hit a clear section along the tracks and touched his heels to the gray. He held the reins loose so the animal could keep its head down. For an hour or more he jogged along the track until he was in the deep timber down off the side of the first bluff. He pulled the gray to a walk as the track curved to the left. The turn had a tight radius, probably the tightest on the hill. It was there that Buchanan stopped.

115

He dismounted and slipped out the crowbar. No one would be stupid enough to ride big, clumsy work horses down the mountain if they could drive the locomotive. Schmidt would do that, and if he could get off the mountain, he could beat Buchanan to the railhead. "I guess we'll just ruin your day, Bert," Buchanan said aloud. He walked down the tracks for another thirty feet until he was sure he was working at the most obscured portion of railbed. The engine would come around the corner without enough time to stop.

Buchanan scuffed snow on the backside of a small drift until his toe hit steel. With the claw of the bar, he cleared away the snow, running the tool along the rail until he came to the end of the section. He set to work in earnest, his arms and back straining. First a spike, then another, and the rail joint plate came free. He worked back along the length of the rail, prying the short spikes back from the track flange. Once the crowbar slipped, smashing his fingers down on the tie. He cursed but continued until only one spike on the inside of the rail was left. With a cry of jubilation, he hurled the crowbar away and raced back to the free end of the rail. With a grunt, he slid the rail sideways toward the end of the ties. He moved it six inches, straightened up, then moved it another three for good measure.

"There, you son of a bitch. Let's see you run your train on that." He smacked his hands together and walked back to his horse. He mounted and looked at his work with satisfaction. The loose rail came after a tight, blind corner, and better yet, was partially hidden by a small drift. If Schmidt did use the train, this was as far as he would get.

Buchanan kicked his gray, then abruptly snapped back on the reins. Five hundred yards down the track were seven riders. Because they were below him, none of them saw Buchanan on the switchback. The big man cursed quietly. He twisted in his saddle, looking behind along the tracks. The riders would see the sabotaged rail. If he stopped in time, Schmidt could spike it back in place, even temporarily, in minutes. He cursed and glanced again at the approaching riders. He saw the bodies then, three of them, tied to the backs of the last three saddle horses in the line.

"Averill," Buchanan breathed. He twisted in the stirrups, scanning the timber along the tracks. If he let them ride close, there wouldn't be any trouble, even with seven of them. He chose a spot and kicked the gray, riding across the tracks. He dismounted quickly and scrambled up through the snow, climbing the steep incline of the track cut. He pulled on the reins and the gray danced sideways, nervous at the slick footing. Finally, the animal lunged, slipped, lunged again.

"Come on, you stupid son of a bitch," Buchanan hissed. He jerked the reins savagely. After another scrambling lunge and a nicker that prompted a string of curses from Buchanan, the gray kicked up to more secure footing. Buchanan made his way up the hill, through the trees, and away from the tracks. When he was fifty yards clear, he stopped, breathing hard. He tied the horse's reins to a sapling, pulled the rifle from the scabbard, and then untied one of the saddlebag flaps. He opened one of the boxes and poured the bright cartridges into his coat pocket. He dumped fifty more into another pocket and then tied the bag shut. The carbine was fully loaded, as was the revolver under his coat. He grinned. He had cover and more than a hundred cartridges. There were only seven men.

He walked back toward the tracks, found a thick stump, and settled down into the snow. With the rifle resting on the stump, he had an unobstructed view of the railbed through the buckhorn sights. He levered a round into the chamber and waited.

Had it not been for the horses, Buchanan would have had no more trouble than a hunter cleaning ducks off the surface of a pond with a scattergun. As it was, he waited until the seven men were no more than twenty-five yards away. When the first man saw the skewed track, he reined his horse to an abrupt halt. Buchanan had the front bead of the rifle on the nearest rider. He saw the rider stop, and he squeezed the trigger.

The heavy .44 slug nearly lifted Homer Cass out of his saddle. The crash of the rifle and Cass's flailing arms spooked the horses. Cass plunged backwards and to his left, falling against Sam Averill's dun. Behind him, Billy Wentworth's horse reared and because of the extra weight putting it off balance, slipped and went down awkwardly. Mike Buchanan levered the rifle and quickly found another target. The rifle blasted again and Milt Holmes screamed and rolled out of his saddle. His horse, with Cyrus Taber's frozen corpse lashed behind the saddle, skittered forward, spinning Sam Averill's mount and saving the rancher's life. Averill dove out of the saddle, landing heavily on his left side in the snow. He rolled off the rail grade, clawing for his handgun at the same time.

Buchanan fired again, this time taking out Fats Sweeney, a veteran rancher who had managed to slide his own carbine out of the saddle boot. With the animals milling, Buchanan hesitated. He saw Billy Wentworth slide out of sight down the hill, and then he swung his rifle as Joey Roberts kicked wildly at his horse, trying to bolt up the tracks. Roberts was no more than twenty yards from Buchanan's rifle when the first slug tore through his arm. He fell forward against the horse's neck and Buchanan fired quickly, hitting the horse solidly. To his left, the one cowhand still mounted had a revolver in hand and managed to snap off a shot that went wild. Buchanan first shot the nickering, dancing horse, and then, as the animal tripped to its knees and Nels Carson leaned back in the saddle to keep his balance, Buchanan fired again. Carson landed on his face in the snow. Buchanan saw Roberts on his feet as his horse staggered away. The ranchhand dove for cover just as Buchanan fired. The slug caught Roberts in the middle of the back, and he tumbled down the slope.

Mike Buchanan sat still, holding his breath. On the churned railbed before him, he could see four men, all motionless. He knew the one who had been knocked over the edge of the slope was no consideration. That left two. Before moving, he reached into his coat pocket and brought out a handful of shells. He slid one after another into the rifle until the magazine would take no more. As he did so, he watched the hillside. No head showed. He glanced up the hillside. His horse was just visible through the trees, unharmed. Buchanan remained seated, thinking hard. He could trail the two men easily enough. They wouldn't get far. But they were armed. If he stepped to the edge of the railbed, he would be a fine target, silhouetted against the sky. He turned his head and looked up the hill. Two saddle horses stood nervously, ears cocked in his direction. Without hesitation, he swung the rifle and fired six times in rapid succession. One horse screamed and went over the side of the railbed, and the other plunged off into the trees.

"Walk, you bastards," Buchanan whispered. With eyes still scanning the hill, he scrambled to his feet and then turned and made his way up the hill to his own horse, loading the rifle as he did so. He was ten feet from the gray when a shot crashed out and a limb near his head snapped bark in his face. He dove to one side, saw his target, and fired.

"Billy, stay down!" Sam Averill screamed. He saw snow kick beside the cowpuncher and Averill snapped off a shot. Both Wentworth and Averill had heard Buchanan retreating through the trees, and they both had scrambled back toward the railbed. Wentworth was about to sprint across the tracks when Buchanan fired, and simply out of reflex, Averill found himself standing in the open to give the youngster cover.

Buchanan's shot at Wentworth had been fired while on the move. He saw the gun in Averill's hand, turned, and fired. The rancher went over backwards, disappearing over the slope. Levering the rifle quickly, Buchanan managed another shot at Wentworth just as the cowpuncher reached the edge, and his lips compressed with grim satisfaction when he saw the slug spin his target nearly a full turn. With a cry, Wentworth disappeared over the edge.

This time, Buchanan wasted no time. He dashed to his horse, grabbed the reins off the blackjack, and plunged off through the unbroken snow. He stayed in the trees, above the tracks, for nearly a hundred yards. As the track turned away from him, he angled downhill, keeping tree cover between him and the carnage above in case one man remained alive. It was only well below the final switchback that he rejoined the railbed, riding quickly toward the south.

XVIII

"MISTER Averill!" Sam Averill heard Billy Wentworth, and he groaned as he tried to push to his hands and knees. "Mister Averill, you all right?" Wentworth was sliding and stumbling through the snow, making his way toward his boss. Wentworth reached his side.

"He's gone," Averill said. "I saw him through the trees, going on down the hill."

"Can you make it up the hill?"

"Maybe." He pulled at his coat. "Hit me in the arm, and then when I fell down the hill, I broke it." He grimaced and held the mangled limb tight against his chest. "How about yourself?"

Wentworth's face was pale and his lip trembled, but he tried for nonchalance. "Lucky, I guess," he said. He pulled his coat to one side and showed Averill his belt. The .44 slug had hit the heavy leather of his holster a glancing blow. Averill was about to speak when he heard hissing and clanking in the distance. He recognized the sound of the train and then remembered the damaged track.

"Get yourself up there and stop them," he snapped to Wentworth. "I'll get up there best I can. Now move!"

A quarter mile from the blind turn, the three men in the engine saw the saddle horse first. The animal was standing beside the tracks, head down. There was no sign of a rider. Phillip Scott was already cutting the steam and setting the brakes when they looked ahead and saw Billy Wentworth staggering and slipping along in the tracks of the horses. He saw the locomotive and began to wave his arms wildly, only stopping when it was apparent that the engine had already slowed to a crawl.

Schmidt felt a surge of relief. "It's one of Sam Averill's cowpunchers," he shouted, and he swung out so that he was hanging from the side of the locomotive with one hand. "Keep comin', keep comin'," he ordered Scott. "Maybe they got him." But as soon as they were close enough to clearly see Billy Wentworth's face, they knew that wasn't so.

"Some bastard bushwacked us from up in the trees," Wentworth shouted as the engine wheezed to a halt. "We never even saw him."

"Where are the others?" Gingras asked.

"Mister Averill's down the tracks a ways. Him and me . . ." He turned with sudden realization. "I never checked to see." And before Schmidt could grab him, he was off through the snow again, racing down the tracks the way he'd come.

"Slow," Schmidt yelled. "Keep it slow." He held the revolver at the ready. Even the logger, hardened by years near dangerous machinery and the threat of constant injuries, was unprepared for what lay around the corner. First a dead horse, and then Sam Averill standing by the track, one arm bloody and useless. He saw four more bodies sprawling in the snow, and more dead stock. The locomotive stopped and he swung down. He thrust the revolver in his pocket.

"They're all dead?" he asked quietly.

"Yes," Averill nodded. "Joey Roberts is over the side there. He's dead too."

"It was Buchanan?"

"I think so. I don't know him well. I caught a quick glimpse of him through the trees."

"He riding a big gray horse?"

"Yes."

"That's him, then. Anyone manage to hit him?"

"Shit," Averill grimaced and spat. For several seconds, words failed him, then he looked hard at Schmidt. "That bastard sat behind that big stump," he said and pointed to the spot. "He waited until we were right where we see Homer Cass, lying over there. Then he started shooting with a rifle." He looked down at the snow. "Slaughter." He glanced at Schmidt again. "Slaughter is what it was. Five good men. Jesus Christ almighty." There were tears in Sam Averill's eyes then. "I want this man, Schmidt. I don't know what drove him to it, I don't give a damn. I want him."

"He won't get far," Bert Schmidt said. "We can catch him before he makes the Union Pacific. That's the only direction he can go."

"We don't have the riding stock to carry us. And you don't have the track," Averill said. "But by God, I'll have him if I have to walk all the way to the Mississippi."

And for the first time, Bert Schmidt saw the damage to the track. He strode forward. Fats Sweeney was lying directly on the loose rail, and Schmidt pulled him free. "Jean-Paul," he said, "get me something from the engine that I can pound with." He walked up the loose rail to the end. "Billy, come here." The two of them slid the rail back in place. "We got one spike back at that end. One on this side is all we need." He bent down and pulled one of the loose spikes on the inside of the rail. It came loose, and Schmidt put it in place at the end of the rail on the outside.

"Jean-Paul, what did you find?"

"Nothing is loose, wait a minute."

"We don't have a minute," Schmidt muttered. He turned, eyes searching. He took several quick steps and bent over Joey Roberts's dead horse. With a grunt, he pulled the old rifle out of the twisted saddle boot. "It'll have to do," he said. He emptied the round from the single-shot's chamber, and then with short, powerful chops, drove the muzzle of the rifle down on the spike head. In a moment, the spike was tight against the rail flange, and the rifle was forever useless. Schmidt flung the gun down the hill. "That will hold the rail all we need for now." He beckoned to Scott. "Let's clear the tracks," he said. As the engine eased past, he said to Averill,

"We'll put your men on one of the flatcars. There's nothing we can do for them now, and there's no time to waste." He swung up into the engine for a moment. He spoke quickly with Scott, and jumped back down. "We've horses in the boxcar, or I'd put the men there," he said, but it was obvious Averill didn't care. He was standing by the side of the railbed, gazing down the hill. When the locomotive was once again ready to roll, Schmidt laid a hand on Averill's shoulder. "Are you going to be all right?"

Averill turned and looked expressionlessly at the logger. "Of course not," he said. With his good arm, he grabbed the handrail on the side of the locomotive and swung up into the cab. Schmidt followed. As if not trusting the engineer, Schmidt leaned forward toward Scott. "No whistle, mister," he said. "The longer it takes Buchanan to learn we made it past his trap, the better."

As the train began to move, Schmidt pointed at the floor of the cab. "Sit down, Sam. I want to look at that arm."

"It's all right."

"It's got a bullet hole through it, and it's broke. That's not all right."

"It'll keep."

"If you want to be alive when we catch up with Buchanan, then let me look at the arm." That logic won out, and Averill sat down heavily on the rocking cab floor. The effort to remove his coat cost him more pain than the wound, a deep gouge below the elbow. Schmidt wrapped a reasonably clean bandana around the gash. "Wrist hurt?"

"Just aches now."

"Then we'd best leave it alone." With his coat back on, Averill leaned back against the cab wall and closed his eyes.

Before they were out of the mountains, Scott was forced to stop the locomotive three times so that the men could clear drifts from the tracks. And each time, Sam Averill stood by one of the windows, gently pounding his good hand against the sill with impatience.

As Schmidt, Gingras, and Wentworth reboarded from one shoveling session, Averill pointed impatiently at the deep trail left by his own horses when they had made the trip from the Triple S to Williams early in the day. "He'll make good time," he said. "Better than we are. And he's got a start on us."

"Only until he reaches the cutoff to your ranch," Schmidt said as the train jarred into motion again. "Then he'll be pushing through unbroken snow. Unless the whole way is blown clear, we'll have the advantage." He paused. "And maybe we'll be lucky. Maybe his horse will throw him . . . break his neck."

"I hope for only one thing, Schmidt. And that is that he is not that lucky."

XIX

MIKE Buchanan was willing to gamble, and his luck held. He was confident that no one was close on his trail—and if someone was, slowing down to look over his shoulder wouldn't improve his chances any. He pushed the gray hard, doubly so when he reached the open prairie. He guessed correctly that if he rode near the side of the railbed, there would be no obstructions under the snow. It was late afternoon, darkness already working as the eastern horizon began to take on a leaden cast. Buchanan figured in simple arithmetic. If the horse broke a leg, he could probably walk the remaining miles to the railhead during the night. It would be impossible to get lost with the tracks to guide him. No one could approach him in the darkness without being heard. He grinned as the sharp air stung his cheeks.

He didn't know the Union Pacific schedule, but there would be a train the next day, one direction or the other. It didn't matter which. There was no telegraph at the railhead, so even when his pursuers did reach the main line, there was no way for them to send messages ahead of the train. His gloved hands relaxed and he let the gray have its head. He reached the turnoff to the Triple S and pulled the gray to a walk. The tracks of Averill's horses led off to the west, and ahead of him stretched a prairie unblemished. The sun was sitting squarely on the horizon, and Buchanan knew he had no more than a half hour of light. The railhead at Littel was eleven miles away. Two hours, without sparing the horse. Or a four hour walk. Either choice, Littel was easily within reach. He glanced over his shoulder, saw nothing but open space. In front of him, blown to a flat monotony of contour,

127

the snow averaged a foot deep. He could clearly see the parallel mounds of the tracks off to his left. He kicked the gray into a gallop and snow was flung in all directions from the animal's flying hooves.

Had Mike Buchanan taken the time for a closer look, he might have seen the faint, distant plume of dark smoke from the locomotive. Finally off the treacherous slopes of Williams Peak and onto the open prairie, Phillip Scott opened the throttle cock. The engine rumbled along at a solid ten miles an hour, bucking once in a while as its cowcatcher sprayed a small drift from its path.

It was dark when they reached the Triple S junction. Schmidt stepped off the motionless locomotive and examined the tracks. He walked on ahead, and then returned quickly.

"He went on to Littel," he said to the others in the cab. "One set of tracks. By the spread of the holes in that snow, he's not sparing the horse any."

"If he doesn't kill the horse, he'll be at Littel in two hours, then," Averill said quietly.

"Yup. There's enough light he can see the rise of the tracks to guide himself. He won't stop."

"And neither will we. Engineer, get this train moving." And Averill stopped suddenly, glaring at Scott. "Then it must have been you," he said, clenching his teeth.

Phillip Scott gently eased the steam throttle open, but he didn't take his eyes off Averill. Schmidt could see what was coming, and he stepped between the rancher and his engineer.

"Leave it be," he said.

"He was running this engine when my men were killed," Averill said. "When Burke and Taber and Payne were gunned down. That means he was in on it."

"That's right, he was, Sam. And I say let it be. It took you this long to realize that, let it ride a little longer. He knows what he did, and we need him." Averill slowly sagged back against the cab wall and rubbed his face with his good hand. After a moment, he looked up and nodded. Schmidt let out a breath of relief.

On Schmidt's instructions, the engineer slowed the train to a walk.

"I don't want to beat him there," Schmidt said. He glanced at Averill. "I want him inside, warm and comfortable. With Dick Smith. I want them both." He tapped Wentworth on the arm. "And keep your eyes on those tracks. You've got good eyes. With this starlight, they should look like postholes." But the tracks didn't vary. The ocean of snow caught even the faintest light, and the prairie took on a hazy, ghostlike cast. Ahead of them, what light there was in the sky was blacked out by the great buttress of Thunder Butte.

They eased along for another hour until they were on the east side of the butte. Schmidt tapped Phillip Scott on the shoulder. "Stop here," he said. As the engine lurched to a halt, he turned to the others. "If we run any closer, there's the danger he might hear the engine. I don't want him running." By the faint light that seeped past the firebox door, Schmidt's face was barely visible. "We take the horses in from here. Scott will stay with the engine and keep the boiler going. Billy will stay as well. There's three horses, and three of us."

Wentworth, over the initial shock of what he had witnessed on the mountain, shook his head. "I'm goin'," he said.

"No, you're not," Schmidt said, "and I'll tell you why. I'd have to shoot your boss here to keep him from going with us, hurt as he is. Now, if we don't come back, somebody's got to make his way to the Triple S to tell them what happened. Scott here will have his hands full. That leaves you, Billy. And if you argue with me any more, you won't be in shape to ride anywhere."

Jean-Paul Gingras was already out of the locomotive, pushing through the snow back to the boxcar. As Schmidt swung down, he looked back at Wentworth. "Think of the bright side . . . you and Scott will be the only ones who stay warm tonight. You've got plenty of wood, and God knows you have the water. Scott, I want that engine at Littel come daybreak. Wait until full light, and then come on in."

Schmidt rode the Belgian. The other two horses were smaller, mixed-breed work horses, almost small enough to be considered stock horses. Sam Averill struggled up into the saddle with a grunt.

"Christ, Schmidt, whyn't you use normal horses?" he muttered in the dark. His words went unanswered and the three set off. None of the animals were high-steppers. They all plodded, scuffing the snow like patient, old men. Because all three animals wore the heavily cleated shoes of timber-country stock, there was no slipping, even in the dark. After only five minutes, the locomotive was just another dark splotch on the night-shadowed prairie. The faint tracks of Buchanan's fast gray led them on.

As the trail began to turn slightly west, around the southern flank of the butte, Schmidt found himself squinting into the cold, still night air for the first lights of the railhead station. Gingras saw them first, a minute, faint, and single glow. From that distance, no buildings could be distinguished.

Schmidt called a halt, and the three men sat quietly on their horses.

"It's still about two miles," he said softly. "As I remember, there's just the one building there where they'd be holed up. That's Smith's station. That the way you remember it, Sam?"

"Yes. There's the station, and then the corral, and over past that, as I remember, there's just a couple of tack and equipment sheds. Just little shacks. They'd be in the main building."

"We'll walk in the last mile or so. I don't want to take a chance on these horses nickering back and forth. I don't remember the building good enough to be able to figure on how to take Buchanan yet. I think we all need to see it close up."

"You just remember that he ain't about to give you no second chance," Averill said. "He's a mad dog if there ever was one. You see him, you shoot him. That's the way I figure it."

Schmidt didn't answer, but he kicked the Belgian forward. As he rode, he tried to envision the small building. He'd seen it fifty times in his life, maybe more. And yet all he could conjure up was an amorphous shape with a door in the front wall. How many windows were there? He couldn't remember. What was inside? He shook his head in disgust.

"I think it's about a mile from here," Schmidt whispered. He dismounted and walked the Belgian to a stout shadow that was a juniper. He tied the reins loosely, knowing the big horse wouldn't bother to wander. Gingras did the same. "You don't need to tie him," Schmidt instructed Averill, and the rancher looped the reins over the cantle. Schmidt took out his revolver and opened the loading gate on the side. He slipped a glove off and felt with his finger tips, making sure the gun was still fully loaded. He heard the action of Gingras's rifle work.

He looked at the shadow that was Averill. "All set?"

"Let's get on with it."

The big horses had made it look easy. The snow reached mid-calf in most places, and occasionally they stumbled through a deeper drift. The tracks of the gray led unerringly toward the faint light of the station, and they kept their eyes on that.

When they had moved to within a hundred yards of the station, they caught motion for the first time. The small building nestled its back into a jumble of boulders. On the east side was a single window, high off the ground. The light that shone through was not bright, but there was enough that when a man walked past the window, they saw the silhouette clearly.

Schmidt heard Averill's breath catch, and he pointed to the left. He drew the other two over to the rocks, almost out of sight of the station. "What's the hold up?" Averill rasped. Schmidt could tell that the rancher was wound tight as a clock.

"Here's what I want," he said. "We got to know what's inside before we make a move. Jean-Paul, I want you and Sam to stay put here for a minute. I'll go on down, take a look, and hoof it back."

"This is no time for some great goddamned plan," Averill shot back. "Let's go in and get him."

Schmidt reached out quickly and grabbed the rancher's shoulder. "You can count the men Buchanan's killed as easy as me," he whispered urgently. "Now you may want to go on in there and get yourself blown to pieces, but I don't." He leaned forward, face to face with Averill. "I want that bastard to face a judge, Sam. I want him to have to stand up in a courtroom and be seen by everyone for what he is. That'll hurt him more than any quick bullet. And then, by God, he'll hang. That's what I want. Now you and Jean-Paul stay here. I'll be right back." He touched his foreman on the arm. "Make sure he stays with you."

As he made his way down along the rocks toward the station, he felt sure Buchanan would be able to hear his heart beating. He forced his breathing steady. At one point, he heard a horse snort in the distance, and then the nervous lowing of several steers. He froze, listening. There was no other sound. From the chimney of the station, a thin ribbon of white smoke rose arrow straight into the air. He moved forward again, pushing through the snow carefully. When he was fifty feet from the side wall of the small building, he stopped again, crouching low, blending his shape with the smaller boulders. He heard a low voice and cocked his head.

Silence. Carefully, holding the uncocked Colt revolver in his right hand, he eased forward. The window was five feet off the ground, part of the dirty, cracked glass obscured by the wooden shutter that had swung half closed. Schmidt edged closer, heard a clank of iron, and the voices again. He sensed a dark mound directly in his path, and began to skirt it when he heard the door of the station yank open.

"If you had coal, you wouldn't always be runnin' for wood," he heard a voice say, and his stomach knotted. Mike Buchanan stepped out through the door and came around the side of the building. He had a coal-oil lantern in his hand, and Schmidt saw that he had walked into the wood-pile. Buchanan trudged toward him, oblivious to his presence.

Because he was watching where he put his feet, and because the lantern cast a small circle of light, Buchanan reached the end of the woodpile, scarcely ten feet from Schmidt, without seeing the logger. He scuffed a clear spot in the snow with his boot and set the lantern down. Schmidt took one step forward. He raised the Colt and thumbed the hammer back. In the still night, the four clicks of the hammer were as loud as if he had announced his presence with trumpets.

Buchanan froze with one hand reaching down toward the pile.

"Move one muscle, make one sound, and your brains are in the snow," Schmidt said quietly.

"Well, goddamn," Buchanan said, ignoring Schmidt's threat. He straightened up slowly. "I thought I was the only one crazy enough to ride at night in weather like this."

"Back up, real slow."

Buchanan turned his head, peering into the darkness. "Damn, you mean you come down all by your lonesome?" He shook his head and stepped backwards.

"Again, clear of the pile," Schmidt said. He moved around

and walked toward Buchanan. "I said back up, Mike. I'm not the killer you are, but by God from this distance, I can't miss."

"Nope, guess you can't." Buchanan retreated and Schmidt picked up the lantern with his left hand.

"Inside," he said. Buchanan turned obediently and trudged back toward the station. Without hesitation, he reached the door and stepped through with Schmidt behind him. The light from a single lantern hanging from a ceiling beam bounced off a set of crude bunkbeds on each wall. Scattered around the small stove were a few chairs and a single, battered table. It was a place that only a man like Dick Smith would call home. He was like the room—small, dirty, and smelly. He sat at the table, cards spread out in front of him.

"We got us some company," Buchanan said cheerfully. He moved away from the threat of Schmidt's revolver, off to the left. Smith's jaw dropped a fraction. "This here's Bert Schmidt from up to Williams. I guess you've seen him from time to time." Almost as an afterthought, he added, "I thought maybe it'd take him a little longer to get down here."

"Shut up," Schmidt snapped. He tipped the muzzle of the Colt toward Smith. "Stand up," he ordered.

"Best do what he says," Buchanan said, a faint tone of mockery in his voice. "I didn't think you was much for gunplay, pal. Dick, you best do as he says before he fumbles around and that thing goes off by accident."

Smith stood, but he came up quick and smooth. For the first fraction of a second, Bert Schmidt did not see the old revolver in the man's hand. In his eagerness, Smith yanked the trigger prematurely. The old percussion gun bellowed, loosing a great ring of smoke. The crash of Schmidt's .45 came immediately after. The heavy slug blasted through the man's Adam's apple, throwing him backwards. He crashed into the stove, spraying blood. In reflex, he fired the old revolver again, which would have finished Mike Buchanan if he had remained still. But even as the first shot rang out, he was diving forward. Schmidt had pulled the trigger, but had no time to recock the handgun before Buchanan smashed into him. The sheer weight of the big man bowled Schmidt toward the opposite wall. He twisted, felt cloth against his gun hand, and fired the Colt. The report was shatteringly loud. For a fraction of a second, his face was unprotected, and a smashing blow numbed him. And then, Buchanan was gone, out the door into the night.

Schmidt pulled himself up and plunged after him. A rifle barked, and then there was another shot. He sprang through the door and almost collided with Gingras.

"Over by the corral. He's headed that way," Gingras shouted. But there was no way to distinguish Buchanan's shadow from the dark mass that was the corral with its hundred head of milling cattle and horses. As soon as they had plunged past the small circle of light from the station, they realized the impossibility of seeing a target. Their breath rasped as they advanced on the corral slowly, eyes straining to catch sight of any motion. The cattle grunted and shifted and then, as his eyes adjusted, Schmidt could make out the higher line of a horse's back. He started to whisper something to Gingras when Averill, off to the left, shouted, "That's him!" His revolver flashed and the slug caught a corral rail and whined off into the night. From beyond the corral, a rifle bellowed in answer. Schmidt heard the slug snap by.

"Down!" he shouted. "Jean-Paul, he's over by the tack shed. Sam, stay down!" Averill stopped his advance toward the corral and crouched in the snow, the bulk of the cattle between them and the shed. "That's where his saddle and rifle were, then," Averill said, and swore bitterly.

"All right, listen to me," Schmidt said, and he pulled Gingras closer with one hand. "There's no way we can charge him. We're going to have to wait. I think if we move around the side of the corral, we can see enough that we can catch motion. We can see if he tries to make a run for it. He can't get to his horse. He's got to wait too." The three men split up. Gingras moved right, Schmidt creeping around the left side of the corral. Because he could not move as easily, Sam Averill remained in place, peering over the backs of the livestock for motion inside the corral, on the off chance that Buchanan could slither past the men undetected and reach his horse. None of the three men were willing to gamble against Buchanan's rifle, even in the darkness. Between the corral and the tack shed were 120 feet of open space—too far to throw a lantern or to sprint unseen, but short range for rifle slugs.

XX

FOR the first half hour, Schmidt was reasonably warm. He sat in the snow, his heavy coat tight around his body, hugging his gloved hands under his arms. As the minutes passed, he found his eyes adjusting to the darkness, and he began to see details that had been invisible before. Then, with a start, he realized it wasn't so much his eyes adjusting as it was the half moon rising up past the swell of the prairie. As the moon rose, the vast snow blanket acted as a reflector. Schmidt stirred uneasily. He could see the small shed now but he had no idea whether Buchanan was inside or crouched on the other side. The large, looming boulders behind assured that the man hadn't slipped out to the rear. But if he could see the shed, it also meant that Buchanan would be starting to pick out details around the corral.

Schmidt drew back until he was sure his bulk didn't form a bulge to the side of the post and rails. As if in answer, he saw several brilliant flashes and heard the crack of Buchanan's carbine. The flashes came quickly, four of them as fast as a man could lever the gun. The cattle in the corral milled nervously. Schmidt heard a ricochet moan off, and he cocked the revolver. One shot from Averill answered, but Gingras held his fire as well. There was no point in aiming at the spot where the flashes had originated. Buchanan wouldn't have stayed still. Averill's voice floated quietly to Schmidt.

"That shed would be full of feed sacks. Ain't much point in tryin' to get a bullet past."

"He's free to crawl back and forth, shoot from either side, then," Schmidt replied.

"Yup." They fell silent.

"Buchanan!" Schmidt yelled. A single rifle shot flashed from the same side of the building, but low to the ground. Several head of cattle just to Schmidt's right shifted, one of them bawling. Two of the dark forms pushed against the rails, and the wood groaned. "There's nowhere you can go, Buchanan. Throw that rifle out of there."

A jocular curse floated across the space, then Buchanan yelled, "You gettin' tired already, Bert?"

"Nope. It's bright enough now, we can spell each other. I'm thinkin' on gettin' a couple hours shuteye right now, over in the station." He paused and let Buchanan digest that. "Nowhere you can go, Mike. Give it up."

The rifle flashed from the other side of the shed, and far behind him, Schmidt heard glass shatter. He turned his head and squinted, trying to make out the station. "Are you a bettin' man, Bert? I'm bettin' I can see well enough to hit you five times before you get to the station house from where you're sittin' in the cow shit there. How about that?"

Schmidt shook his head wearily. Buchanan was right.

"What do you say, Bert?" He chuckled. That laugh triggered Averill, and the rancher thumbed off a shot.

"Sam," Bert Schmidt hissed. "Save the shells. The cattle are getting riled."

"This ain't as easy as you thought it might be, is it Bert?" Buchanan chuckled. "You fellas is stuck. I got me some surprises, too." He fell silent, and forty yards away, the hair on the back of Schmidt's neck tingled. "Yeah, I got me some surprises." He said that as if preoccupied. "You got down that mountain a tad quicker than I expected."

Schmidt struggled to his feet, staying in a crouch, and backed around the corral. He passed Averill. "Keep a watch," he said, and worked his way around to where Jean-Paul knelt. Buchanan started talking again.

"You find a way to bring the train on down? Or'd you ride that big dumb horse of yours, Bert? Nah, you must have took the train, or you wouldn'ta made it here until a week from Sunday." He laughed again.

"What do you think?" Schmidt whispered. Gingras didn't move.

"At this point, mon ami," the Frenchman said quietly, "I do not know. There is no way across to that building without being a sure target. We know how this man shoots. Maybe I can make it up through the rocks, circle around . . ."

"No. There's no risk to the situation the way it is. Other than spending a damned cold night. I think we ought to wait. Maybe see what he's got in mind."

"I think he has nothing in mind."

"Bluff, you mean?"

"Yes. I see nowhere for him to go. He is surrounded."

"He doesn't sound worried by that."

"That is because he is crazy," Gingras said dryly. Without risking exposure any more than necessary, Schmidt pulled himself up so that he could see under the top rail of the corral—just over the backs of most of the cattle. What he saw was simple enough. The small shed, perhaps twelve feet wide and eighteen feet long, nestled right back against the boulders that had rolled off the flanks of Thunder Butte. To the left, the rocks curved around until the line passed just behind the station house. To the right, across a hundred and fifty feet of flat, featureless snow, lay the spur of the narrow-gauge, and immediately beside that, the slightly elevated roadbed of the Union Pacific main line. Across the tracks the vastness of the open prairie offered no cover, and without a horse, no option.

"You gettin' kind of cold yet, Bert?" Buchanan called. "Whyn't you just stand up and stamp your feet some, heh, heh. My God, you're going to be stiff before long. Me, I got all these old feed sacks wrapped around me . . . snug, my, I'll say. But you, I just bet you're gettin' stiff, eh, Bert?"

"He is mad, mon ami," Gingras said. In the distance, what

sounded at first like a coyote broke the stillness. The sound, high pitched and exquisitely mournful, lingered in the air. Schmidt held the barrel of the revolver up as he listened, every fiber of his body tense. For another two or three minutes, the prairie was silent. And then, again the sound, a single long note that held, and held, and then died, followed by a short tap in the same pitch.

"I'll be goddamned," Schmidt muttered. "Coming in from the west."

"If it should stop here . . ." Gingras began.

"It will. Buchanan knew the train was due, because Smith must have had a timetable. First thing they would have done when Buchanan got down here was go out and set the flag to tell the train to stop."

"He will never make it out to the train," Gingras said. "If he shows his face . . . as bad as we shoot . . . it would be suicide."

"He's got to know that." The train whistled again, and this time the sound was strong. "Trip the flag, and the train won't stop. This isn't a regular water pickup." Schmidt was on his feet, bending low. "Come to the other side, cover me." Gingras followed him. They passed Averill. "I want cover," Schmidt said shortly. With the three of them clustered at the track side of the corral, Schmidt looked quickly across at the white rails. "I'm going to try to get across the main line. The bed is high enough to offer some cover. I can worm my way up-track."

"I don't think there is time," Gingras said, but Schmidt cut him off.

"Cover me." With a powerful lunge, he dashed out into the open, moonlit gap. Although it was only a few feet, to Schmidt it seemed miles. No shots came from the shed, and the logger sprinted through the calf-deep snow, pumping hard. He hurled across the tracks and dove into the snow on the other side, gasping. He lifted his head. He could see no light coming down the track, and he began his belly-low flounder. He had no clear notion how far up the track the flag was, but he realized that whether the train stopped or not, his new position would be a great advantage. Buchanan would be pinned down from two directions. He drove hard with elbows and knees, head down with his face more in the snow than not. He heard the shrill whistle again, and glanced up. Faint, still more than a mile or more in the distance, he could see the headlantern of the big engine. The train wouldn't be moving fast, he thought, not with the snow. Twenty, thirty miles an hour, maybe. Maybe a little less, with the slight upgrade past Littel.

He stopped and looked back. He'd covered more than a hundred feet. He couldn't see the flag. If it was five hundred yards, he would never reach it this way. He drove on, and when he thought he had covered two hundred feet, he raised his head just enough to see over the roadbed. The light was such that the shed was visible, but no detail below its overhang on the rock side. Gritting his teeth, he sprang up and raced forward, crouching as low as he could while maintaining his balance as he crashed through the snow. The train whistle let out a shriek at the same instant that something sparked off the iron rail just in front of Schmidt. He heard the boom of the rifle, then several sharper cracks. The locomotive's head lantern was bright, gently oscillating from side to side as the engine rocked on the tracks. Without breaking stride, Schmidt leaped across the rails. He realized perfectly well that he was giving up protection, but he trusted to the distance. He did not want the train between himself and Buchanan.

All he could see was the glare of the lantern. He would never reach the flag. And as he thought that, he heard the first squeal of brakes as the engineer saw the flag and began his stop. Schmidt stopped, panting, bent forward at the waist. The light loomed large, and this time, the whistle was ear-piercing. Schmidt waved his arm frantically, and then cringed as he heard a slug ricochet off the engine.

"Don't stop!" he screamed at the top of his lungs. He dove

forward again. The engine was traveling at no more than ten miles an hour when the huge, iron bow of the cowcatcher split the coat of snow on the tracks beside Schmidt. The long boiler glided by, steam jetting from the drive pistons, and then Schmidt was looking up at the side window of the cab where a puzzled and apprehensive face peered carefully.

"Don't stop!" he shouted again, and the engineer looked up the tracks. With one arm gesticulating wildly, Schmidt pointed the revolver at the engineer and shook his head.

The engineer was not about to argue. In the middle of the night, in the middle of the snow-swept prairie, he needed no convincing. Littel was worth no argument with a madman waving a handgun. The drive wheels spun and protested as he rammed the throttle home. Black smoke poured out of the stack, and out of reflex, the engineer reached up and hung on the whistle cord.

But even over the noise of the accelerating engine, the vollies of gunfire were vicious. Schmidt could see no rifle flashes from the shed . . . that meant Buchanan was on the far side. But the effects of his gunplay were evident. The cattle were banging and crashing in the corral. The two or three saddle horses there whinnied. The rifle fire continued and was answered by Averill's revolver. Schmidt began his move back, staying as low as he could, hoping the dark bulk of the train offered enough confusion that Buchanan couldn't see him. In seconds, it became apparent what Buchanan had chosen for his target. The cattle were frantic, knocking horn and hoof and belly against the corral poles.

And then the corral collapsed as Mike Buchanan knew it surely would. The animals streamed out to freedom, milling in all directions, but confused on the one hand by the repeated gunfire into their midst and on the other by the growing brightness of the locomotive on the main line. The engineer saw the corral go down, and did the only thing he knew . . . he pulled the whistle cord. The steam shriek sent the cattle into full-blown stampede in all directions.

With that as cover, Mike Buchanan broke away. For such a big man, he moved with grace, heading straight across the now-trampled white snow toward the train. Schmidt saw him, and doubled his pace. There were more shots, two from Gingras's rifle. Buchanan's dark figure leaped sideways, but kept running. Schmidt stopped and aimed the revolver, felt it buck in his hand.

Behind the engine and tender were two boxcars and then a flatcar loaded high with lumber. Buchanan aimed for the flatcar, and when he reached it, there were five cars between him and Schmidt. With a powerful leap and grab, Buchanan in one coordinated movement paced the train and made his bid. One hand shot out and grabbed the chain on the front of the car. For a moment it seemed that he had lost his balance. Then he flung his other hand up and grabbed, finding purchase on the lumber. He instantly swung his legs up. Schmidt aimed and fired again and again. He might as well have been throwing stones. The dark shape that was Buchanan pulled fully onto the lumber, hunched and clawed upwards. He wanted the cover of the lumber, and lacked scarcely two feet of clearing the top.

As he reached for the chain where it crisscrossed the top of the load, his feet flew out from under him. It may have been the slick surface of the green lumber under his boots—perhaps a rifle ball too close. Whatever the cause, he lost his balance with a crash. He made a frantic grab and missed. Schmidt saw him somersault against the edge of the car. And then his figure disappeared.

Schmidt raced up the tracks. A steer dodged out of his way. By now, the train had picked up speed and the wheels were flashing by. Unsure of his footing, Schmidt stopped, eyes searching. Five cars rolled by, then six, seven, and eight. Finally, the caboose, and the tracks were empty. Almost immediately, Schmidt saw the dark shape beside the tracks, lying diagonally on the slope of the railbed. Instinctively, he hesitated, his gun coming up. The clatter of the train was fading and he ignored the cattle. Something in the snow caught faint light, and Schmidt saw the rifle. He bent and picked it up.

He saw a hand move, a jerky motion. Buchanan let out a small gasp and a single curse. With another slight movement, Schmidt could see two hands . . . and nothing held in either one. He stepped close and cocked the revolver.

"It's over, Mike," he said. "You aren't going anywhere."

There was a moment of silence, and Buchanan's voice, when he spoke, was weak. "You can bet that. I broke somethin'. Ain't never fell like that before. I think I broke my back."

"Hangman isn't going to care much one way or the other," Schmidt said, and then he heard footsteps in the snow. Gingras reached his side.

"He is dead, then?"

"Nope. Busted up some, but not dead, Where's Averill?"

"He is coming."

"Watch him. And we've got to figure some way to get this son of a bitch back to shelter. I figure we can drag him right enough."

Buchanan groaned something, and Schmidt ignored him. "Sam!" Schmidt yelled, and the rancher answered immediately. He appeared, limping heavily, the snow almost too much for him to fight.

"Me and a damned steer crossed paths," he muttered. He saw Buchanan. "He dead?"

"Nope."

"Well, he's gonna be," and it was only the rapidity of Gingras's reflexes that saved Buchanan from a bullet. He grabbed the revolver in Averill's hand.

"After all this, Sam, you're not to deny me the pleasure of seein' his face in a court of law."

"Let him have his way," Buchanan said. "I ain't going to make it to no court, anyways."

"We'll see about that," Schmidt said. He and Gingras

grabbed the big man's heavy coat and the two of them dragged Buchanan to the small station. The lantern still burned faintly, but the stove was cold. As they released Buchanan, he sank back on the floor, face staring at the ceiling.

"I can't feel my legs," he murmured.

"Can't help you," Schmidt said. "Even if I wanted to." Averill stood in the doorway, and as Gingras turned up the lantern, Schmidt saw the look of hatred on the rancher's face.

"You ain't going to take me back up that hill," Buchanan pleaded. "I can't do that."

"Help me take this one outside," Schmidt said, indicating Smith's stiff corpse. Then with the room partially set to rights, Schmidt searched for and found the timetable.

"Train for Canyon City comes through here at noon. Says so here." He tapped the sheet. "There's a sheriff there, and there's a doctor there. Don't see as we need more'n that."

"Listen, I can't make no train trip."

"You can, and you will. If all you can do is sit in a chair, you'll hang. I'll see to that."

Buchanan's eyes shifted from face to face, and there was something that could have been fear there. "You wouldn't put a man through all that, Schmidt. I know you better'n you know yourself." He glanced over at Averill, then back at Schmidt. "I know you better. It'd be a favor to all of us if . . . if you'd let that man have his way." Averill's eyes squinted, and then he crossed his arms.

"Buchanan," Schmidt said, "I don't owe you any favors. And these men sure as hell don't. And you'll live, believe that. You may hurt some, but you'll live . . . long enough for the courts to hang you." He turned to his foreman. "Jean-Paul, I want you to ride into Canyon City with him tomorrow. See that the sheriff gets all the details. I'll tell your wife, set things straight with her. Then I'll have the train run back down to pick you up."

"What about Mister Scott?" Gingras asked quietly.

Schmidt rubbed his chin. "I figure to have Buchanan here do something he's never done before."

"I do not understand."

"I figure that Buchanan's going to pay another man's debt for him. By the time we get shut of this one," and he nodded at the pale Buchanan, "I guess we'll be as square as we'll ever be."

XXIII

CHRISTMAS day of 1886 dawned crystalline and cold. No wind stirred the pines and firs of Williams Peak or the mounds of powder that cloaked the village below. Smoke from each chimney wafted straight up into the eye-aching blue of the sky, then gently drifted on the air currents up into the crowns of the evergreens. The temperature stood at twelve degrees above zero when Bert Schmidt rose to stoke the fire and make his entry in the diary.

Juteau and D'Arlene would need no help in the kitchen that day. To even offer would have offended their fragile pride. But Schmidt wanted to make sure the chowhall looked its best. The timber crews had spent much of the day before decorating. Dense, long-needled sprigs of pine were matched with the smaller fir boughs over each window and door lintel—even over the kitchen door that protected the serving counter. There were a few boughs of evergreen on each table, despite the complaints of one of the loggers, a bachelor, that "there ain't no room for the food!" Another had persisted, however, replying that "that's the way it's done." And so it had been. Someone had actually trekked out into the cold of the woods and found a spot on the backside of Williams Peak where the snow wasn't so deep and the grape holly leaves were bright red splotches in the rocks. He brought back enough to grace each table. Then, because others had admired his good fortune and persistence, he was sent out again to scour the lower limbs of the pines for mistletoe. Undaunted, he found some and returned a hero. The doorway to the chowhall was complete. Not a single wife or sweetheart was allowed into the chowhall that Friday.

That was also traditional. No wife or sweetheart would have dared ask if her assistance was either wanted or needed. To a woman, they pretended that their men were off to another working day, like any other. They all knew better. It was Bert Schmidt's tradition that Christmas was celebrated by a gathering. Thanksgiving, Easter, even Independence Day, were private affairs, Schmidt maintained, to be celebrated privately and at home. But Christmas—that was a special day. No one argued with him.

As Schmidt entered the chowhall shortly after seven on Christmas morning, his eyes drifted to the crowning touch. In the corner opposite the woodstove, where tables had been pushed clear, stood the crown of a Ponderosa pine. Two days before, it had graced the very top of a 150 foot giant. After Schmidt had selected the tree by dint of much neck craning, his timber crews had carefully prepared a bed for the tree's fall. Other lesser trees had been cleared away so the tearing of limb against limb wouldn't strip the monarch. When the tree fell into the deep snow, its crown whistling through the air like a giant feather, it hit the bed dead center. Each year before, he had chosen a fine specimen. This year was no exception.

On Christmas morning, Schmidt stood inside the door and looked at the tree. Bright bits of cloth, small and delicate wood carvings, papers covered with the drawings of children, and yards of bright yarn decorated the tree.

"Good morning, Mistair Schmeet," Juteau called when he saw his boss.

Schmidt turned and smiled. "Morning. Smells good in here." Even D'Arlene smiled thinly, then turned to tend his ovens. Schmidt walked to the tree and set the packages down that he had brought from his cabin. They were in the same wrapping paper that weeks before Henrietta McDowell had so skillfully applied. He pushed them further under the tree, smiling to himself. He had visited the widow woman several times in the past few days, and he felt twenty years younger.

From his coat pocket he drew out a thick packet of envelopes and looked at the tree. Carefully he drew the envelopes, one by one, from the packet and balanced them in the needles of the tree. Soon the tree was dotted with them. It was the first year he had done such, but 1886 was a different year from most.

In the kitchen, the two cooks glanced at him from time to time, plainly puzzled. Finally, Juteau could stand it no more. He stood in the doorway of the kitchen, a large wooden spoon in his hand. "What is it you do?"

"Don't know," Schmidt replied. He grinned at the cook. "Lost my head, I guess." That puzzled Juteau even more, and he rejoined D'Arlene, mumbling in French. When Schmidt finished, he stood back and admired his work. The tree looked a mite cluttered, but it couldn't be helped. He patted his pocket, feeling the one remaining paper. It would stay there until the right time.

He pulled out his watch. "You men need anything?" he hollered across the hall to the cooks. Juteau waved an impatient hand, and Schmidt left the chowhall. He went to the stables and gave the Belgian a thorough brushing, thankful again that it had not been that animal, aging and loyal, that had stopped Buchanan's bullets.

When the Belgian was well-brushed, Schmidt harnessed him to one of the smaller wagons. The trail down the hill into Williams had not improved but Schmidt hardly noticed. He pulled the wagon up in front of Carlotta Webster's front door and jumped down.

She answered at the first knock. "I'm a bit early," Schmidt said, and grinned like a small boy.

"Then you shall have to wait," Carlotta answered sternly, and began to close the door. At the expression on Schmidt's face, she burst into laughter. She held the door wide open. "Come in. Come in." She then stepped close and held his face in both her small hands. "You don't know how happy I am that you are having this Christmas of yours."

He held her by the shoulders then and kissed her lightly on the forehead. She hugged him tightly. "There's a surprise or two for you up the hill," he said quietly and she pushed herself away and clapped her hands.

"And I have a surprise for you!" The package she handed him was small, and he hefted it in his large hands, eyebrows furrowed.

"For me?"

"No. For that wonderful horse of yours. Of course it's for you, silly. Open it."

"Maybe I should wait."

"For what. It's Christmas morning. Open it!"

He did so, clumsily tearing the flimsy paper. He held up the finely carved pipe, rolling the polished bowl in his fingers, delight on his face.

"Where'd you ever find this?"

"I ordered it made," she said. "From whom is a secret. Do you like it?"

He looked down at her. "It's wonderful." For several minutes, he couldn't think of anything else to say. Then he rested a hand lightly on her shoulder. "If you'll fetch your wrap, let's go up on the hill."

Carlotta sat close to Schmidt, her arm linked through his, and their laughter joined with the sparkle of the snow where the sun glanced off each delicate facet.

When they entered the chowhall, both Juteau and D'Arlene tried not to stare. Carlotta was stunning in her long dress of red calico with the matching ribbons in her hair. Ignoring their stares, and standing in the open doorway with the bitter air flowing inside, Schmidt pointed at the mistletoe. "You know about that," he said flatly.

"I know about that," Carlotta replied. Schmidt kissed her lightly on the lips, then put a hand under each elbow and lifted her off her feet. He turned and set her inside.

"There," he said, and closed the door. He glanced at the kitchen, then walked over and reached up to the door latch.

He swung the door down, closing off the kitchen. The cooks smirked but didn't argue.

"Such a tree!" Carlotta said with delight. She swept over to the pine, her eyes bright. "And what are all these?" she asked, stepping closer and touching the nearest envelope. She cocked her head and read the name. "Who is Shorty Jenkins?"

"Works for me."

"Why, there's a name on each," she said. "Whatever is in them?"

Schmidt ducked his head in embarrassment. "Oh, a little something. I figured this year was a little special. I gave each of them a week's pay."

She turned and looked at him. "That's very nice," she said softly.

He shrugged. "Seemed like the proper thing to do. But say, there's something under that tree for you." He reached down and pulled out the packages. "Not much, but I hope you'll like it."

Her delight with the gloves, mittens, and scarf was complete. She clasped them to her breast with joy, tears in her eyes. She grabbed Schmidt in such a hug of wild joy that this time he gasped in surprise. She blushed at his reaction.

"Don't worry," he grinned. "I'll get used to it." He kissed her hard. For many minutes they stood, holding each other tightly. Schmidt rested his face against her thick hair, smelling the fragrance that to him was sweeter than any of the decorations or the delectables being prepared in the kitchen.

"I have another surprise, and you'll be the first to know."

She pulled her head back and looked up at him. She saw the serious expression on his face and her pulse quickened. He reached into his pocket and pulled out a paper. "I want you to read this."

Puzzled, she took the paper and unfolded it. She read it quickly and at the same time felt a tightening in her stomach that was keen disappointment. She had hoped for something else, had hoped with all her heart and soul, for she had made up her mind days before about the course her life would take should she be given the choice.

Bert Schmidt watched her eyes move as she read the paper, and he kept his face impassive. "What do you think?"

Carlotta looked up into his eyes and tried to keep the tremor out of her voice. "I think," she whispered, "I think that you are the most generous man I have ever known."

He took the paper from her and folded it slowly. "It isn't generosity," he said, looking at the note in his hands. "Jean-Paul doesn't have a penny, except what he earns here. He's got a wife, two little ones. With all that, he never blinked when he went south with me. And when the shooting started, I couldn't have asked for a better man. He wasn't doing it because he takes pay from me, Carlotta. He did it because . . . because he's a good man. A good man, Carlotta. They're not so common these days."

"And so you're giving him a partnership in the mill."

"I am. He's earned it. I've been thinking about it for some time. I'd just about made up my mind. Now I'm sure."

"He should be a happy man."

"I sincerely hope so." He read the expression that lay deep in her eyes. "And so will I be. I'm doing it out of self interest, you understand." She started to say something, but he laid a finger across her lips. "Maybe I'm not being the gentleman I should be," he said, still holding his finger to her lips. His voice was sober. "It isn't much more than a month since . . ." He paused. "It hasn't been much more than a month, but I've made up my mind. I intend to give Jean-Paul the responsibility of the mill because I intend to be busy doing other things." A smile spread across his face. "I want to spend the spring doing a job pretty dear to me, and doing it proper. There's this young lady I sure hope won't take it unkindly if some old, beat-up, broken-down logger came courting."

Carlotta Webster had never fainted in her life but just then she thought she would. Tears flooded down her face and she embraced Schmidt with all the strength she had.

At that moment, the door of the chowhall burst open and two loggers stepped inside, stamping the snow from their boots. They made it no more than two paces before they saw their employer doing something they had never before witnessed. By God, he was kissing a pretty woman. But they only had time for a quick gawk, for the door of the kitchen flew open and Pierre Juteau advanced on them, wooden spoon in hand. His French was eloquent and far from Christian, but the two immediately understood and re-treated.

"One o'clock!" Juteau shouted. "One o'clock! You do not come in here before that time!" He verbally pushed them out of the hall and slammed the door, marching back toward the kitchen, still cursing. He reached the door and turned briefly. Both Schmidt and Carlotta were wide-eyed with astonishment. He waved the spoon at them and winked, then closed the kitchen door behind him.

EPILOGUE

ON January 9, 1887, every demon in the western sky rebelled. A north wind shrieked down from Canada, building a storm of mammoth proportions that lashed the ranges from the Yukon to New Mexico Territory. Snow hurled across the mountains and prairies.

For ten days the blizzard continued. On January 15, the temperature dropped to forty-six below zero in Williams. Not one out of a hundred cattle on the open prairie survived the onslaught. People hardly fared better.

By the time the storm had exhausted itself, all the coal in Williams had been burned and all the beef in the ice house had been delivered to families who had no way of replenishing their dwindling supplies. The missions of mercy were not without cost. The storm killed ten people in Williams alone.

After resting for slightly more than a week, the storm returned with renewed fury, blasting the ranges for a full seventy-two hours before losing interest in the cattle that stood frozen against fences or in the false protection of trees and gullies. The major herds on the open ranges were broken, but the ranchers who were still alive counted themselves lucky that they would be able to try again.

It was early March before Sam Averill and his men were able to tally their losses. Of the three thousand head of cattle, Averill could count the survivors on one hand. If he took any satisfaction in the storm at all, it was in learning that Mike Buchanan would never face the compassion of the courts. The train taking him to Denver for trial in federal court had been stalled on the tracks as the snows swept across, burying the rails and the engine. The few other passengers and the

crew had managed to stumble to the safety of a small ranch
house during the early morning hours of January 28. They
huddled and waited for the storm to break itself. They had
not been able to move Buchanan on his stretcher, and he had
frozen to death as the hissing storm covered the train with
snow.

If you have enjoyed this book and would like to receive details of other Walker Western titles, please write to:

Westerns Editor
Walker and Company
720 Fifth Avenue
New York, NY 10019